The
Betrayal

Also by Mary Hooper

Historical fiction

At the Sign of the Sugared Plum
Petals in the Ashes
The Fever and the Flame
(a special omnibus edition of the two books above)
The Remarkable Life and Times of Eliza Rose
At the House of the Magician
By Royal Command

Contemporary fiction

Megan
Megan 2
Megan 3
Holly
Amy
Chelsea and Astra: Two Sides of the Story
Zara

The
Betrayal

MARY HOOPER

BLOOMSBURY

LONDON BERLIN NEW YORK

Bloomsbury Publishing, London, Berlin and New York

First published in Great Britain in 2009 by Bloomsbury Publishing Plc
36 Soho Square, London, W1D 3QY

A CIP catalogue record of this book is available from the British Library

ISBN 978 0 7475 9910 4

FSC

Mixed Sources

Product group from well-managed
forests and other controlled sources

Cert no. SGS - COC - 2061
www.fsc.org
© 1996 Forest Stewardship Council

Typeset by Dorchester Typesetting Group Ltd
Printed in Great Britain by Clays Ltd, St Ives plc

3 5 7 9 10 8 6 4 2

www.bloomsbury.com/childrens
www.maryhooper.co.uk

Contents

Chapter One

The second week of January was so fearsome cold that hoar frost edged the bare twigs of the trees lining the lanes and even the deepest puddles iced over. Beth, Merryl and I, waiting endlessly with others on the turnpike road which ran from Richmond to London, pretended we were dragons to pass the time, huffing out our breath in great clouds of vapour.

We were waiting for Her Royal Majesty Queen Elizabeth and her court, who were leaving Richmond Palace that day for the Palace of Whitehall in London. They were moving to give Her Grace a change of scene, and also to ensure that Richmond Palace was aired and freshened after being occupied by hundreds of people for nigh on three months. On the roadway with us were scores of loyal neighbours and citizens, all of us mighty sorry to see her go. This wasn't just because the Royal Court brought prosperity and vitality to the area, but also because we loved having our beloved queen living in close proximity to us, knowing that at any moment she might be seen riding with a pack of hounds into the great park or glimpsed gliding downstream on the royal barge. We were privileged indeed to live, for at least some of each year, so close to the lady we all loved and revered.

Merryl sighed, tiring quickly of the dragon game. 'Will she be much longer, Lucy? I'm so cold!'

'Any minute now,' I said. I crossed my fingers against the Devil catching me out in a lie. 'I'm sure I hear the wagons rolling . . .'

I tucked Merryl's shawl more snugly around her and told both children to march up and down like the queen's soldiers in order to warm their toes. They sighed again, but were obedient girls and so, stamping furiously, they began marching along, cresting ridges of mud which had been hard-frozen into icy peaks and breaking them into powdery lumps.

'How can she take this long to get ready when she has at least forty maidservants to help her?' Merryl asked as she stamped.

'About one maidservant for each garment!' Beth said. 'And have you thought that when she *does* come, she'll go by us in a moment wrapped in so many furs that we may not even see who's in the centre of them.'

'I'm sure she will not,' I said, 'for Her Grace likes to be seen and admired by us. And even if she *is* too muffled in her ermines and her bearskins, there will be many other grand ladies and gentlemen of the Court to set our eyes upon.'

As I spoke I looked down the road once more for any sign of the cavalcade. I spoke of other grand folk, but really I was thinking of one person in particular: Tomas, who was the queen's fool and would be travelling with Her Grace's trusty band of jesters, clowns and jugglers. Tomas was my special friend. *Friend*, I thought firmly, and not sweetheart, for I mustn't let the one kiss there had been between us permit me to think there was any understanding. At least not yet. In time, though, I dreamed there might be, for I was sure that he liked and admired me.

'We've seen all the gentlemen and ladies of the Court before, though,' said Beth plaintively. 'And anyway, the queen often comes to call on us and when she does we have her all to ourselves.'

'Hush!' I took a quick look around to see if anyone else had heard this, for some Mortlake folk were nervous about being in close proximity to those of us who lived in the house of the queen's magician, thinking us all conjurers and dabblers in the black arts. The reality, however, was very different, for although I hadn't been working as a nursemaid at the house for very long, it was obvious to me that Dr Dee was somewhat lacking in those dark skills said to be necessary for someone of his calling. He was supposed to be able to contact spirits – but once, failing to do this, had paid me two gold coins to pretend to be the wraith of a girl who'd died. On another occasion I'd been taught – by trickery and sleight of hand – how to substitute base metal for gold so that it would look as if my master had found the secret of the philosopher's stone. He was, without a doubt, tremendously skilled in languages, map-making and charting where the stars were positioned, but I'd not seen anything in the least bit magickal while I'd been working at his house.

Merryl frowned at her sister. Two years younger, she was a girl as dry and sensible as a dowager. 'Her Grace is not *always* visiting,' she corrected. 'She came exactly twice last year. Once to ask about an elixir and once to ask Papa about the witch doll someone had . . .'

'Hush,' I said again. 'You know your father doesn't like you to speak about his work outside the house.'

Beth gave a great sigh and surveyed the distant road once more. 'Perhaps she's changed her moving day again.'

'It's packing up all those precious jewels that's taking the time!' a grimy farmer standing alongside us said with a chuckle. 'I heard she had so much gold and so many gems as New Year gifts that she could have opened a shop and traded as a jeweller.'

I smiled and nodded by way of reply, knowing that the man spoke truly. This was because I'd been lucky enough to be at the palace on New Year's Day and had seen the costly gifts piled and tumbled on the table, awaiting her attention.

I looked down the road now, surveying those waiting to see Her Grace. They were mostly working folk: gardeners straight from Mortlake's asparagus fields, two or three burly blacksmiths, brewers, lightermen and bargemen from the river, goodwives on their way to market, two stinking night-soil men (people were placing themselves a way off from these) and a fair sprinkling of apprentices, maidservants, cooks and housekeepers from the big houses. We'd all assembled on the roadway a few days previous to this: two days after Twelfth Night and the day the Court had been due to move, but then the message had spread down to us that there had been a change of plan and that they wouldn't be travelling until this morning. Mistress Midge, who was cook and housekeeper at the Dee house, had elected not to come again, saying she'd got quite cold enough the previous time.

'I hope Her Grace is not unwell – it's not clear why they didn't move on the first day,' I said to the farmer.

''Tis probably nothing but the whims of majesty,' the farmer said. His nut-brown face creased in an indulgent smile. 'Her Grace looks out of the window and decides it's a little too chill, so Her Grace decides to leave it another day or so before she travels.'

I smiled. 'The poor Lord Chamberlain will be near-fainting with despair.'

'Why will he?' Beth asked.

'Why? Because he will have arranged long ago for the queen's refreshment stops and her comfort breaks, and instructed the towns along the way to tidy their streets and form their children into choirs of angels to sing to her as she goes. And all these tasks would need messengers sent to change their arrangements at the last moment.'

'Aye,' the farmer said. 'The money that the nobility spend to entertain her on her progresses! I heard that an overnight stop at the Lord Taverner's house last year cost him a year's income.'

I nodded. 'And I've heard of a great house built in anticipation of a royal visit which never happened! But today they hope to make it to London before nightfall, do they not?'

He nodded, then gave a shiver and rubbed his calloused hands together. 'Though if they are much later in starting 'twill be midnight afore they bed down.'

'Have you ever been there – to London?' I ventured.

'Me? Been in London?' he asked, then spat on the ground. 'No, I have not, and I take pleasure in saying so.'

'Indeed?'

'Aye. They say 'tis a wicked and corrupt place, where folk would stab each other for a penny, and a man may be forced to beg on the streets for his daily bread.'

'I have heard the very opposite!' I said, laughing. 'I have heard that London is like a great storehouse of things to be enjoyed; of taverns where the wine flows all night, of lavish suppers and of merrymaking, of theatres and dancing.'

'Mayhap. If you've got the money and your face fits,' said the farmer. 'But what would there be in London for the likes of me?'

'I think I can hear something!' Beth said suddenly, and she ran off to a bend in the roadway and was joined there by her sister.

'I can see some horses,' Merryl called, jumping up and down on the spot.

'And noise! I can hear cheering!' Beth shouted back to me.

'They're coming at last!' came several voices from the crowd. 'The queen is on her way!'

'God be praised,' said the farmer, 'for my toes are frozen past redemption.'

More than an hour later the procession was still going past us. We'd seen dozens of horses, scores of litters and I cannot tell exactly how many laden carts but 'twas a great number, for Merryl counted to over one hundred of these before she got muddled. It was only right and proper that there were many and varied conveyances, of course, for these carried the trappings of majesty and ensured that wherever Her Grace went she would be surrounded by the splendour necessary for the greatest sovereign ruling over the mightiest nation in the world.

We'd noted the humbler palace staff pass by on foot, and seen, too, the highest royal servitors: the maids of honour and the ladies of the bedchamber, followed by the gentlemen of the Court – titled nobles all, their insignia glittering across their manly chests, their hat plumes waving and stirrups a-jangling as they rode their magnificent horses. As yet, however, there had been no sign of Gloriana.

I looked down the lane, craning my neck to see into the distance, eyes searching in vain for her white palfrey with its jewelled saddle and bridle. She must be here somewhere, for it was unthinkable that the Court would leave without her. Could she be masquerading? I wondered. Might she have gone past us dressed in a lowly servant's garb, playing some sort of game which would prolong the seasonal fun? I knew that masquerading was something that the Court – and Tomas especially – enjoyed very much, for he'd often caught me out in one of his jests. But surely, I thought, Her Grace wouldn't hide herself away on a journey to London, for she knew her subjects would be lining the streets and she loved being seen by them, receiving their shouts and acclaim and returning their greetings.

Some ten carts from the royal kitchens went by: a welter of roasting spits, kitchenware, pots and pans, tankards and gilt plate, and then there was a lengthy pause in proceedings. After this the cry went up, 'The jesters are come!' and I excitedly set my side curls to rights under my hood and hoped that my nose wasn't too red nor my cheeks too pinched with cold, for now I would see Tomas, and he would see me.

'Now comes Tom-fool!' Merryl shouted excitedly

(for, being the queen's fool, this was the name by which he was usually known).

The decorated cart carrying the jesters trundled slowly towards us. It held the Greens, a family of five, who each had their own particular skill. They smiled broadly and acknowledged the shouts of the crowd but, despite being entreated, did not undertake any juggling or clowning. On the cart beside them were two monkeys and the queen's dwarf, Thomasina, who was much loved by everyone and thus got a tremendous cheer and calls of 'Greetings to the little lady!' Of Tomas, however, there was no sign.

'Where's Tom-fool?' Merryl cried, disappointed, for she and Beth were very fond of him and had met him several times when he'd come a-visiting Dr Dee's house with Her Grace.

I stared after the cart. 'I don't know,' I said, perplexed. Perhaps he'd gone by us in one of his disguises . . . but surely he wouldn't pass without a wink or a wave to me? Perhaps he had some malady? But then I'd seen him only a few days before, when he'd kissed me goodbye and told me that he'd see me soon in London, for, to my great excitement, Dr Dee and his household were due to follow the Court and take lodgings close to Whitehall.

Another pause ensued, then a large and sumptuous litter came by, borne aloft by four gentlemen-at-arms, one marching at each corner. The litter was hung with purple velvet curtains, shut tight, and bore the royal insignia and shield.

The crowd around us fell silent and the farmer and I exchanged puzzled looks.

'Three cheers for Her Majesty!' he shouted after a moment's hesitation, and the people around us responded with cheers and applause.

As these fell away everyone fixed their gaze upon the curtains, confident that they'd open and a royal hand would appear and wave in acknowledgement. It did not, however, and the litter proceeded silently on its way, leaving a puzzled crowd in its wake.

Why had Her Grace not acknowledged the shouts when she loved showing her glittering self to her people? Was she really inside, or were the gentlemen carrying an empty litter? Did she – perish the thought – have the smallpox again and, being disfigured, not wish to be seen? These questions, and many others, were murmured, discussed and answered piecemeal as more and more carts came by.

'But now comes Tom-fool on a horse!' Beth cried suddenly, pointing. 'At least . . . I think it is him,' she added with some uncertainty.

I stared where she was pointing. Over the months that I'd been working as a nursemaid in the Dee household, I'd seen Tomas in various disguises, a grinning cat one day, a Harlequin or Jack Frost the next. These disguises, he'd explained to me, were not only part of his role as fool in the royal household, but also meant that his face was not recognised when he was going about his other duty: that of working for Sir Francis Walsingham, that nobleman known as the queen's spymaster. It was in this role that I'd come to know him best, for unbeknown to anyone bar my friend Isabelle, I'd been asked to assist in simple little spying tasks which a girl of my station might quite naturally undertake: listening at doors, following a certain person, making discreet enquiries about this or that. I very much enjoyed doing these things, for they were all in the service of our lady queen. Thinking on this, I touched the little coin I wore at my throat. It bore the queen's image and though it was but a humble and tawdry thing (which Tomas oft teased me about), such was my devotion and loyalty to Her Grace that I'd worn it since I was a small child.

Now I strained to see if it *was* Tomas trotting towards us. The rider had a pretty falcon hawk chained to his wrist and was clad in a hunting jerkin of worn brown leather, the hood of which was pulled well across his face. This guarded against a sharp beak nipping his cheeks and might also, perhaps, prevent onlookers from getting too close a view of his face.

The glance of the youth on the horse fell on me, and I smiled. It *was* Tomas, I was sure of it, for even though his face was shaded I could see his grey eyes flickering silver in the half-light. I waved.

'Tomas!' the girls called. Then, 'Tom-fool!'

I wondered afterwards whether or not he'd intended to stop anyway, but just at that moment one of the kitchen carts ahead rolled into a large rut in the road. There was a creak and a crack and its wheel came off, thus causing the cart to be thrown heavily to one side and the whole procession behind it to come to a halt. Seeing this, Tomas must have thought it an opportune moment to fly the falcon. He released its chain and flung it high into the air, where it hung a moment, then began to circle effortlessly above us.

'Do get down and speak to us, Tom-fool!' Merryl said. 'We have been waiting an awfully long time.'

Tomas smiled at them. And at me, I like to think. He glanced back and I saw, for the first time, that his horse's bridle bore a long cord, which led in turn to the bridle of the small white pony behind him. A girl was seated on this pony, a girl with glossy dark hair spread like an overcape across her wool gown of Tudor green. She wore a pink feathered cap on her head and I caught a glimpse of pink velvet boots under her gown.

I have heard before of love at first sight, and believe it possible. If one believes this, then surely the opposite can be true: that you mislike someone at first sight. Was it just her appearance? I wondered afterwards. Perhaps if she'd been a plain girl, a dumpy creature with a face like a penny loaf and hair as dry and straggled as a horse's mane, I might have liked her better. As it was, she was very pretty and I did not. And I especially did not like the cord which tethered her to Tomas.

'We have here a new lady-in-waiting and a nervous

rider,' Tomas said, seeing my glance. He smiled at the girl. 'We will stay here just a moment.'

''Tis of no matter,' the young lady said, 'for it's a relief to me when my pony stops moving.' She laughed and swung back her hair. 'I am more used to being driven in a carriage, but swear I would rather walk to Whitehall any day than ride about on this beastie!'

I forced my cold face into what might pass for a smile, but need not have bothered because she wasn't looking at *me*, a mere nursery maid; her gestures and glances were all for Tomas. My mind began to chase a hundred different questions: was she at Court to find a rich husband? Where had she come from? Who was her sponsor? Would she – oh, lucky girl! – become one of those chosen confidantes of the queen? Would she settle down at Court or not? Perhaps she would miss her mother and ask to go home again.

'Tom-fool!' Merryl said. 'Will you do us some tricks?'

Tomas shook his head. 'Today, my children, I'm not Tom-fool.' He beckoned them close and added in a whisper, 'Today you see me as one of the queen's hawk-meisters.'

'Then will you bring your bird down to see us?' Beth asked.

He nodded. 'In one moment.' He looked towards me. 'And how do you fare, Mistress Lucy?'

I smiled as carefree as could be. 'I do very well, and thank you. Though we are frozen to our bones from waiting here so long.' I dropped my voice, 'But can you tell me why Her Grace has gone by huddled inside her litter and not shown herself to the crowd, for we are all very concerned.'

He shrugged. ''Tis nothing. She's merely taken a chill and prefers not to expose herself to the frosty air.'

I stared at him. I have one accomplishment which oft-times serves me well, and that is: I sometimes have feelings about things. My friend Isabelle says I have the Sight, but I don't like to call it that, for they say similar gifts are possessed by witches. By some strange and unaccountable means, however, I knew that Tomas wasn't speaking the truth. 'Do you say so?' I asked, rather coolly, for I had proved in the past that my loyalty and love for the queen were unquestionable, and I did not care to be fobbed off with trite excuses as if I were just anyone.

'Ah.' He knew I didn't believe him. His eyes flickered around us, making sure no one was close enough to hear his next words. 'Very well – but I must be brief,' he said in a low voice. 'You remember the so-called secret which was actually the talk of the Court?'

'Which one?' I asked, for the Court is ever a seething mass of rumour, mystery, gossip and speculation.

'The rumour which concerned the queen's favourite.'

I nodded immediately, for Isabelle and I had been quite agog with the tale of the Master of the Queen's Horse, Sir Robert Dudley, long held to be her lover, who'd recently wed without her knowledge or consent. 'Has she found out about the marriage?' I asked, for the last I'd heard, none of her ladies-in-waiting had been able to bring themselves to tell her of it. 'How did that happen?'

'A few days ago – the rightful day we should have set off for London. Her Grace was told of it out of spite by a foreign ambassador after she'd refused his own marriage proposal.'

'Never!' I exclaimed. Behind Tomas's back I was aware of the white pony frisking about and the girl on its back making noises of annoyance. 'And Her Grace has taken it very badly?'

He nodded. 'She has. She has wept so much she says she's not fit to be seen by her people. Hence she travels behind curtains.'

Tears sprang to my eyes. 'Poor lady! I think she really loved Sir Robert.'

'Indeed. She says her heart is broken.'

'Then . . . ?' I didn't have to finish the question, which was one oft asked: *why hadn't she married him?*

'Because he's not popular with her senior ministers,' said Tomas, shrugging. 'There was the difficulty with his first wife dying in a suspicious manner . . . and anyway, the queen's ministers want her to add to her status and her coffers by marrying a rich foreign prince, not give herself to someone as comparatively low born as he.'

We fell silent for a moment, then there was a shout

ahead of 'Wagons, roll!' from the driver of the repaired cart.

The young lady on the white pony gave a little cry. 'Tomas! By your leave we should depart. My pony grows impatient.'

I glanced at her. Did she wonder for just a moment who Tomas was speaking to, or had she looked at me, summed up my lowly status and presumed he'd stopped to amuse a simple maid with his falcon?

'At once!' Tomas leapt back on to his own horse's back, pulled at the cord to bring the white pony closer and flicked it on the nose. 'Be steady, my boy, or you will unseat your little mistress!'

Beth came up and tapped his leather boot. 'Don't forget your falcon!'

Tomas looked up at the sky and gave a long, low whistle, causing the bird circling above us to fly down. Reaching into his jerkin pocket Tomas pulled out something small and dead, and threw it into the air. The bird swooped upon it and swallowed it in a gulp, then resumed its place on Tomas's gauntlet to applause from Merryl and Beth and others nearby us in the crowd.

I smiled at the display, but thought only of the queen; our poor, heartbroken queen.

Tomas gave me his hand in farewell. 'We will meet in London,' he said formally.

I bobbed him a curtsey and extended this to the young lady on the pony, spreading my skirts and dipping very low, for she was of the nobility.

She didn't acknowledge my courtesy, however, for she was sharing a joke with Tomas, and when I straightened up their horses had joined the vast, winding trail of travellers going towards London. Above the noise of the crowd I could hear the clip-clop of their hoof-beats and her laughter, tinkling on the chill air.

Chapter Two

I could think of nothing but Tomas all the way home, despite reproving myself for doing so, reminding myself yet again that just because he'd paid me some attention it need not mean a thing. At Court people kissed, flirted, paid lavish compliments and even wrote sonnets to each other just as means of passing the time.

Things were very different in Hazelgrove, the little country village where I'd been brought up. There the choice of sweethearts was few, and a girl would usually marry a boy she'd known from the cradle. Life there was quiet, my sisters were fully grown and had left home, and I'd worked every day with my ma making gloves for the gentry. Nothing very exciting had ever happened to me – until I'd run away.

I'd run away, I reflected, still amazed at myself for having dared do such a thing. I'd had no real alternative, though, for I regret to say that my father is a drunken, violent brute, and my choice was between staying in the village and continuing to be bullied by him, or leaving home. I'd chosen to leave and – save for missing my ma – had never regretted it for a minute.

As we neared the magician's house the wind began to blow off the Thames, cold enough to make us gasp.

'Will it snow today?' Beth asked as we huddled further into our shawls.

I looked up at the sky, which was darkening, but not with the leaden tinge a snowy sky usually takes on. 'I don't think so.'

'If it does, can we make blocks of it and build an ice house?' asked Merryl. 'Then we can make snowballs and keep them until next July.'

'If you wish,' I said, smiling, for with all the extra padding against the cold she was wearing, she was as round as a snowball herself.

We turned into the lane running alongside the river to reach the back door of the house, for only Dr Dee's clients went in the front way.

'Did you think that lady was pretty?' Beth asked.

'Oh, *very* pretty,' Merryl answered immediately. She looked at me. 'Did you think she was pretty, Lucy?'

'Whoever do you mean?' I asked.

'The new lady-in-waiting!' they chorused.

'I can't say I noticed.'

'I liked her pink boots and cap,' said Merryl.

'They call that *cerise*,' said Beth. 'I expect that's the

latest colour from Paris.'

'But *velvet*!' I said, and sniffed. 'Velvet is hardly practical in this weather. One spot of mud and those boots will be ruined.'

They both looked at me curiously. 'I thought you didn't notice her,' Merryl said.

'Things like getting your boots marked don't matter if you're a real lady,' said Beth, 'because you'll have a maid to clean them for you. And anyway, she'll probably get picked up from her pony and carried into the palace, so she won't have to tread in any mud.'

'Yes,' Merryl nodded solemnly. 'I expect Tomas will carry her in.'

They both looked at me again and I forced myself to smile and say that he probably would do, and yes, now that I'd thought about it, the new lady-in-waiting was quite passably pretty.

Letting ourselves in the kitchen door we found Mistress Midge sitting with her feet up in front of the fire. Mistress Midge is a large and rather dishevelled woman, her stockings bagging around her ankles and her dress and apron covered in spots and blotches of this and that – so much so that our meals for the last week might well have been discerned from a careful study of them. It was most unusual to find her sitting quietly before the fire, for she has a fidgety nature and hot temper, and these things usually combine to make her a woman not often to be found in a good humour.

The girls' pet monkey, named Tom-fool after the jester, was in the grate, as close as he could get to the fire without being burned, holding out his little monkey-hands to the flames. I looked at him pityingly; I was not at all sure where monkeys came from but reasoned it must be one of those countries with palm trees and hot sunshine, so the poor animal must have been feeling the cold dreadfully.

When I'd first come to live in Mortlake it was not long after Beth and Merryl's little brother had been born and the whole house had been in a topsy-turvy mess, for the nursemaid had run away with the valet and several other members of staff had walked out. At first I thought they'd gone because they hadn't been paid, but – although this must have been a factor – Mistress Midge maintained that it was also due to the fact that, knowing they were working for a magician, their imaginations had run away with them. In other words, they'd looked into dark corners and seen wraiths and ghosts where there were only cobwebs and shadows. Mistress Midge, at that time, was acting as the Dee family's cook, housekeeper, parlour maid, house-maid and nursemaid. Her only help was that small amount given by Mistress Allen, who was Mistress Dee's companion (and who rarely left the upstairs rooms), so I'd come along at just the right time.

As I began to divest the girls of their outdoor clothes, Mistress Midge turned to me, her forehead and cheeks red from the fire and her hair as unkempt as a lark's nest. 'The doctor and Mr Kelly are in the library and have asked not to be disturbed – and Madam's gone to see the babe,' she said, meaning that Mistress Dee had gone into Barnes in order to see her youngest child, who was still with a wet nurse. 'You might think I'm just sitting here in front of the fire, but I'm working,' she said self-righteously, 'for I'm thinking of all the things I'll need to take to London.'

'Have you heard when we're going?' I asked eagerly, for now I knew Tomas was on his way there, that day couldn't come quickly enough for me.

She shook her head. 'It'll be when Dr Dee says so, I reckon. When he's secured a place for us on a barge.'

'In a moment I'll begin making a list on one of the children's slates,' I said (for Mistress Midge could neither write nor read). 'And then we can be quite sure that we don't forget anything.' I took off the girls' shawls and cloaks, then their hats, hoods and high pattens, the removal of all of which made them shrink down to near half the size they'd been outside.

'You're not really going to London without us, Lucy?' Beth said plaintively. 'However shall we manage?'

'Your mother's companion can look after you girls,' Mistress Midge said, adding in an aside to me, ''twill show the lazy harpy what hard work is all about.'

'But why have you got to go?'

'You know the answer to this,' Mistress Midge answered Beth. 'Your father is taking lodgings so that he can be close to the queen in Whitehall, and Lucy and I are to go ahead and get it ready for you.'

'But why can't we come too?'

Mistress Midge kicked at a log with her foot to prevent it falling out of the fire, making the monkey jump for his life amid a shower of sparks. 'Because the lodgings have previously been rented to ne'er-do-wells,' she said. 'Besides, there's scarce any furniture there. Some must be sent for, and some purchased, and all must be put in order, ready for your arrival.'

This removal of furniture and purchase of new stuffs, I thought to myself, was going to cost a considerable amount of money, and money was not something that Dr Dee usually had much of. From standing outside doors and listening to gossip (for I own I am of a very curious disposition), I knew that Dr Dee's position at Court was not one which earned him a regular sum, and the amounts of money he charged for explaining dreams and casting natal charts mostly went on books for his library, which I had heard said was the most extensive in England. He had, a few months past, earned an amount of gold for the seance at which I'd appeared as a dead girl, but this money would not last long, so I'd deduced that he was following the Court in the hopes of obtaining more rich clients. He also hoped that the queen would give him patronage until he found that miraculous object which all alchemists seek: the philosopher's stone.

'Did you see Gloriana?' Mistress Midge asked.

Beth shook her head. 'We saw the royal litter,' she said, coming close to the fire to warm her hands, 'but the curtains were closed and she never peeped out.'

'We saw Tom-fool the jester,' said Merryl.

'He was with a very pretty lady-in-waiting,' added Beth.

I clapped my hands briskly to change the subject and to guard against any possibility of debate about that lady's prettiness. 'Now, girls, go and get your horn books,' I said. 'You must practise your letters so that when Mr Sylvester begins your lessons again you can show him how diligently you've been working.'

Obediently they cleared a space at the big table in the kitchen and ran to find their books – which took some time, for they hadn't used them at all over the festive season and things had become misplaced.

I took off my outer clothes and left my pattens and boots by the back door, then joined Mistress Midge in front of the fire. I longed to speak to her of the queen but knew that I must not – and besides, my feet were so aching with cold that I felt I could have cried. I wiggled them, screwing up my face in agony, and Mistress Midge glanced down.

'Why, your toes are quite blue!' she said. She reached up to the string running across the front of the fire and took down some rags and old pieces of towelling. 'Take these old cloths and wrap your feet up in them,' she said, and I did so, tying them with string around my ankles so that I appeared to be wearing steamed puddings on my feet. The girls laughed and I did, too. They might not be as elegant as cerise velvet, but they were warmer.

We hadn't been back in the house more than half an hour when the bell in the library rang. Mistress Midge had started dinner by then so I said I'd answer it and, first taking off my pudding-feet and putting on my house-shoes, made my way along the dark corridors to see what Dr Dee wanted. As I did so I reflected how quickly I'd become used to the house and its secrets. When I'd first arrived, I'd felt intimidated by the doctor and his library – indeed, I'd not even known what the word *library* meant – and finding myself in it for the first time had been overawed at the amount of learning embodied by the books and terrified by the trappings of magick about me. Now, however, I was able to walk into this room almost as easily as I walked into the kitchen. But I knocked first, of course, went in and bobbed a curtsey, then waited to be told what it was they required.

Dr Dee, very much as usual, was in a world of his own and hadn't registered my presence. He was not a tall man, but he cut an imposing figure, with white hair and a beard so long that it almost met the furred cuffs of his clerical black gown. He was standing behind his desk, staring at the strange object he held before him: the black mirror through which he purported to contact the dead. He frowned, murmuring under his breath as he twisted it this way and that, endeavouring to catch the reflection of a candle and then direct this light in turn on to a parchment. This paper, as far as I could see, contained numbers set out in intricate tables: a great many of them, writ very small. These, Beth had once told me, had all been received by Mr Kelly from the spirits and painstakingly transcribed by Dr Dee. Beth also said that once the key to translate these coded messages was found, it would lead to miraculous discoveries.

I looked with interest at the mirror (for it did not often come out of its box), and strained my ears to try and determine what Dr Dee was muttering, but his voice was too low and also some of his words seemed to be in a foreign language and were thus unknown to me.

Mr Kelly, his long-term partner in the magickal arts, was standing behind Dr Dee, eyes closed, arms stretched out to the desk as if allowing some unseen power to flow down his arms and on to the parchment.

Neither of them acknowledged me and my glance slid away and beyond them, to the tall stained-glass window with the Dee coat of arms on it, to the stuffed birds and animals, the turtle shells and sea shells, the gnarled tree roots and – most of all – to the hundreds of books. How could anyone in the world need so many books?

Mr Kelly suddenly turned. 'Girl!' he said (for he never called me by my proper name). 'Don't just stand there gawping.'

I gave another curtsey. 'What can I get you, Sir?' I asked.

'You can bring me and Dr Dee a glass of malmsey. In fact, bring a bottle!'

There was a murmur of protest from Dr Dee, who was no doubt thinking of the cost.

'Nay!' Mr Kelly said. 'We need some fortification for our endeavours.'

I turned to go but, as I reached the door, Dr Dee's voice suddenly rose. 'Spirits!' he called. 'Through this dark mirror shine your light on our work and let us receive entirely the knowledge that you have already blessed us with!'

'So be the will of Ariel!' cried Mr Kelly.

I hesitated for just a moment, loath to leave in case some magick was about to happen, but Mr Kelly realised I was still there and, with an angry gesture, bade me begone.

But I knew it was not very likely that I would have seen magick anyway, and thinking on this, I went back to the kitchen to fetch the malmsey.

That night, I had a most realistic dream about Tomas and the lady-in-waiting, during which she – who'd hardly glanced my way – had curtseyed low before me, as if I was the lady and she the serving wench. I'd had this type of dream before: clear and uncomplicated instead of blurred and unreal as recalled dreams usually were, and tried not to pay too much heed to them, for sometimes – occasionally –

they'd predicted things in my future that I'd rather not have known about. *This* time, however, I very much enjoyed revisiting my dream, and went on enjoying it for several days after.

Chapter Three

The hard frost passed but, while I waited to hear when we'd be going to London, the days seemed grey and dreary. Every day I thought about Tomas and could not help but imagine him and his new lady friend becoming closer and more intimate. In my mind's eye I saw them riding together, making music, dancing and reading poetry; genteel pursuits which a maidservant might hear about but have no true knowledge of.

A week or so after the Court left for Whitehall the day seemed especially drear, so I decided to take the girls for a walk on Barnes Common and call upon Isabelle to share my gossip about the queen. Mistress Midge refused to have the monkey left with her as he'd taken to pulling her hair, so he had a bonnet placed on his head by Beth and, swaddled warmly in a woollen shawl, allowed himself to be carried along like a babe in arms.

Isabelle's home was very humble – even more so than my own home in Hazelgrove – being a hut composed of wattle walls plastered over and shuttered windows without glass. There was a fireplace, but no proper chimney, so whenever the door was opened it caused the smoke to billow and engulf the occupants within. It did this as Isabelle's mother came to the door in response to my call, along with four or five chickens which she quickly ushered back inside. She smiled at me, then dropped a curtsey when she saw that I was accompanied by Beth and Merryl, knowing that these were the children of the queen's magician.

'Your mistress has a new baby?' she said in surprise, looking at the bundle carried by Beth.

I shook my head, laughing. 'She gave birth some months ago – but that's not the child.'

Beth held up the bundle to her and Isabelle's mother, seeing his funny little monkey-face, started back in surprise.

'It's a monkey – the children's pet. He's quite harmless,' I added.

'Indeed.' I saw her glance go over the garments that the children were wearing and then she looked down at herself, pulling her shawl down over her patched kirtle in an effort to hide it. 'Some children have dogs as pets, and some have kits, but I've not heard of anyone having a monkey.'

As the smoke blew past us I heard Isabelle's little sister, Margaret, coughing. 'But I mustn't keep you,' I said, 'I just came to see if Isabelle is quite well, for I've looked for her in the market these days past and haven't seen her.'

Isabelle's mother shook her head, nervously fiddling with one of the ties of her jacket. 'No, she's not been out a-selling, she's been laid up for some days with a dizziness in the head.'

'Oh. Is she . . . still poorly?' I asked, trying to peer through the darkness and the smoke of the cottage to see if Isabelle was within.

'No, she was feeling a little better today, and has gone out.'

I turned to go. 'So will she be at her selling space in the market?' I asked, for this was where Isabelle was usually to be found.

She shook her head. 'Today she's gone to church to be a mourner at a funeral.'

I was not surprised at this, for Isabelle was mistress of all trades and it was nothing for her to be trading in the market one day, working as a washerwoman the next and collecting pots in a tavern on the third.

'Is that in Mortlake?'

'No, at St Mary's in Barnes. 'Tis one of the nobility being buried,' she added, 'and Isabelle has been given a new pair of black leather gloves and a length of costly black muslin she must drape about her head.'

'Then I'll go and see if I can find her,' I said, and set off across the common with the girls beside me, thinking that a funeral – especially if it was a member of the

39

gentry who was being buried – would be a curious thing to see.

On the way across the common Tom-fool got tired of playing a babe in arms and, escaping from the swaddling, pulled off his bonnet and threw it into a tree. He then began leaping across our shoulders, trying to pull off each of our head coverings in turn. Luckily, sensible Merryl had brought some string to use as a lead and we slipped this around his collar so he couldn't completely escape from us.

The only people standing outside the church when we arrived were two ostlers holding the reins of the glossy dark horses that had pulled the funeral carriage. This was standing, empty, in the lane. I didn't intend to go into the church (I could well envisage the mischief an excitable monkey might wreak on the solemn offices of a funeral service), so we stood in the graveyard, reading out the epitaphs on the stones while we waited for the service to be over. There was a yew tree planted by the gate and Tom-fool slipped his string leash, leapt into this and began to climb to the top.

Through the closed door of the church I could hear the minister speaking, though couldn't make out his exact words. When he stopped, there were several moments' silence and then the bells began tolling. Hearing this and knowing the service was at an end, I retreated with the girls behind the churchyard wall to watch the rest of the goings-on.

It was immediately clear that someone from a noble

family was involved when the church doors opened and two grand aldermen in black-and-gold gowns appeared carrying staves and bearing wooden shields painted with a coat of arms. After these came two heralds with banners, then four men wheeling a kind of hand-carriage, upon which rested the coffin, this being covered with a glossy, black velvet pall, heavily fringed in gold and bearing the same arms. The family followed behind (two women, both crying, and many men), then the paid mourners. These consisted of twelve boys of graduated heights all carrying painted wooden shields, and twelve girls holding billowing black feathers. They were clothed and veiled identically so that I could not tell which girl was Isabelle.

'I think it's someone from the Walsingham household who's dead,' Beth said in a whisper. 'I recognise the colours of his coat of arms.'

'Are you sure?' I asked, and before the words were half out of my mouth saw the stately figure of Sir Francis Walsingham, whom I recognised from Court, emerge from the darkness of the church dressed from head to toe in black velvet. Some passers-by had gathered to watch the cortège move in procession through the graveyard, and I ascertained from a stout goodwife that it had indeed been a relative of Sir Francis who'd died.

'It was only a distant cousin,' she whispered, 'but he bears the Walsingham name and so must be buried with all due ceremony.'

'He was young?' I asked.

'I believe he was twelve.' She pointed towards the mourners. 'There are two times twelve mutes for each year of his life.'

I nodded. 'My friend is there amongst them.'

'And my son!' she exclaimed proudly. 'There he is, one of the smallest. He's earned himself a fine pair of leather gloves, a black cloak and a silver sixpence today.'

I murmured approval.

'He's near nine years old, but passes for five or six because he's so small. He's much in demand for children's funerals.'

'And are all the other mourners local children?'

She shook her head. 'They couldn't find enough of the right size, so they had to hire them from Christ's Hospital. Such a fuss and bother! The children all came down by cart late yesterday and had to sleep in a farmer's barn the night.'

'What is Christ's Hospital?' I asked curiously.

'Oh, 'tis a home in London for orphans and foundlings where they hire out the children for any occasion. 'Tis grim there, by all accounts. I tell my own lad that if he misbehaves, that's where he'll end up!'

We watched in silence as the coffin was lowered into its final resting place. By this time my girls were complaining that their hands and feet were cold, and Tom-fool must have felt this too, for he returned, shivering, from the yew tree and crawled under

Merryl's shawl to warm himself.

The minister began to speak again and, seeing that the paid mourners remained in the church porch, some distance from the family, I took the opportunity to go and speak to Isabelle. It did not take long to ascertain which was she, for one of the veiled shapes dropped their pious demeanour on seeing me and smiled and waved.

'Don't tell me that you've come to say goodbye,' she said after greeting me.

I shook my head. 'I have not – not yet. I still don't know when I'll be going to London.'

'Well, I'm glad of that,' she said. 'I know you're anxious to see your Tomas again, but I shall miss you very much.'

'And I shall miss you,' I said, squeezing her hand. I looked across to the funeral party. 'Will you be finished here now that the corpse is in the ground?'

She shook her head. 'We have to accompany the party home – and then we can attend the funeral feasting after.' She lowered her voice. 'The family generally have no appetite, so there'll be plenty to eat.'

She was standing beside a small child. Like the other boys, he was dressed in black doublet and breeches, with a black cloak on top. On his head he wore a close-tied black linen coif with earpieces, such as old men wear to their beds, and this gave him an odd, animal-like appearance.

The boy rubbed his stomach. 'The feasting is the

best part! There will be capons and rabbits and roast swans!'

'There may be,' Isabelle said cautiously. 'But sometimes the family think it more appropriate that we fast, thinking that our aching stomachs will help us look more mournful.'

The boy groaned. 'Never!'

I smiled at him. 'I've just been speaking to your ma. Is that her over by the churchyard wall?'

He shook his head. 'Nah, Missus. Ain't got no ma – and no pa either.'

'You must have had at one time,' I said.

'Not me! Left outside Christ's Horspiddle, I was!'

I looked at him more closely and saw that under his hood his hair was cropped very short, workhouse-style. 'You are one of the foundling boys?' I asked.

'That's right, Missus. And when we gets back it'll be too late for vittles, and Matron takes our sixpences off us *and* our new gloves and cloaks, so all we'll be left with is what we've scoffed. If we don't get nothing here I'll starve.'

I was about to sympathise when Merryl waved her hand to draw my attention. 'We are both very cold!' she hissed at me accusingly, so I quickly bade goodbye to Isabelle, saying that I'd be in the market place the next morning and that we could talk then. 'I have much to tell you about the queen,' I said in a low voice.

Isabelle's eyes gleamed. 'News of Her Grace? I shall see you tomorrow!'

44

The little boy pulled at my hand. 'Are those two girls yours, Missus?' he said, nodding towards Beth and Merryl.

'Do I look old enough for that?' I said, smiling. 'No, I'm their nursemaid.'

'And do you all live in a big house together, with their ma and pa and so on?'

'We do.'

'Well, ain't that nice,' he said, and turning to the girls, he gave a little mock bow in their direction.

I patted his head, forgetting how much little boys hate this and causing him to scowl at me. 'I hope you get some vittles,' I said.

I glanced over at the family mourners before I left the church. The two ladies had retired into their carriage but a dozen or so gentlemen – including the imposing Sir Francis – were standing about the newly dug grave while the minister gave his eulogy.

I bade farewell to the goodwife and the girls and I set off for home. I didn't find out until later that someone was watching intently to see the direction we took . . .

Chapter Four

The next morning, Isabelle heard my story of the queen and Sir Robert Dudley, gasping with surprise all the while.

'God save us all!' she said when I'd finished. 'And what do you think will happen to Sir Robert now?'

'She'll take away all his privileges, no doubt. And for sure she'll ban him and his new wife from Court.'

Isabelle nodded. 'Perhaps she'll look again at her list of suitors and choose one to marry to make Sir Robert jealous.'

'Perhaps she will,' I agreed. 'They say foreign princes surround her like bees about a hive.'

'But do you think she'll ever marry?' Isabelle mused. 'What she seems to enjoy best is having a parade of dashing suitors competing for her attention with expensive presents and jewellery.'

I nodded and could not help but smile, for we were

talking once more of our favourite subject: the queen and her would-be lovers. 'But once she's chosen someone, then the compliments and gifts and gee-gaws from all the others will stop coming, and she won't like that a bit!'

I'd found Isabelle at her usual place in the market, selling onions. There was a wooden crate full of these in front of her, all nicely rounded, looking firm and of a good colour. Behind her, however, there was another crate and some of these were misshapen, some sprouting, some with a greenish tinge. Whenever a housewife stopped in front of the stall, drawn by Isabelle's strident call of 'Fresh and strong onions!', she would proffer one of the good onions to feel and then, if the housewife wanted to buy, serve her from the other box (but with such clever sleight of hand that they did not see that they'd been hoodwinked).

I asked if she'd eaten well at the Walsingham's funeral breakfast.

'We did not eat at all,' she said indignantly. 'We followed the empty carriage back to the Walsingham estate – 'twas a goodly walk – but were sent packing with our sixpences before we'd hardly glimpsed the house. We went home with empty stomachs!'

'Then the little boy I spoke to didn't get his roast swan?'

She shook her head. 'Someone came along, herded all the Christ's Hospital children into a cart and took them back to London.'

'Shame!'

She nodded. 'Off they went with rumbling stomachs and many complaints.'

'It must be hard to live in such a place as they do. They can't get much care and attention.'

'But 'tis better than being on the streets,' Isabelle said. 'Sonny – for that was the name of the boy you spoke to – told me that he'd lived a year or more in an empty beer barrel, coming out to beg his food by day and creeping back into it at night-time.'

I was shocked. 'Do you think that true, or was he just saying it to gain your sympathy?'

She shook her head. 'There are many who live like that in London – that and worse. I heard of two sisters who slept all year round on the foreshore of the river and had to move themselves every time the tide came in.'

''Tis much harder in a city,' I conceded. 'At least a homeless child around here could find a hedge to sleep under, or double up with the animals in a barn.'

A housewife came up to be served and insisted that she be allowed to pick and choose her own onions, so I left Isabelle to it and went home.

There I found Mistress Midge in a high old flap and much more like her usual self, bustling about, swearing under her breath, throwing utensils and crashing pots around for no good reason.

'What do you think?' she said. 'You and I are to go to London the day after tomorrow! Dr Dee has secured us a place on a hired wherry going downriver, and we are to be taken as far as Puddle Dock – which is supposed to be close to the new lodgings.'

I felt a great surge of excitement.

'But how we are supposed to get there with all the stuffs we have to take, the Lord only knows. Boxes of books for the master, household pans, linens for the bedchambers and bits of this and that – there is no *end* to it. I don't know how two bodies can achieve it, indeed I don't!'

'What are the lodgings like?'

She shrugged. 'Shabby, I should say, for no one has lived in them for some time. Someone has offered them to Dr Dee, however, and as long as they are cheap and near enough to Whitehall, that's good enough.' She gave a snort of derision. 'And no matter if we have to work our fingers to the bone scrubbing, scouring, brushing, cleaning and making ready!'

'When will the family follow us?'

'Just as soon as we have near-killed ourselves getting things nice, I suppose.' She took a deep breath. 'But the mistress has just discovered she's with child, so she may want to take a little more time about it.'

'She is *again* with child? But the babe is only . . .' I counted on my fingers, 'four months old.'

'These things happen.' She shrugged. 'And she's not feeding Arthur herself. That might have safeguarded against another pregnancy.'

'So that's why she didn't seem to recover from her

lying-in,' I said, for the mistress was weak and had hardly moved from her rooms all the time I'd lived in the house.

'That will mean two Dee babes with a wet nurse by the end of the year – that won't be cheap.'

Interesting though this line of conversation was, my main concerns were how I'd fare in London and how quickly I'd see Tomas. 'How long do you think we'll stay in the city?' I asked.

She shrugged again. 'Lord knows, and the Lord's not telling. Now where's that list of things we must take?'

For the rest of that day we were in a rush and a flurry, fetching and carrying things from Dr Dee and the mistress and packing them in boxes. Dr Dee supplied some old documents in order to wrap the kitchen bowls, and I studied them carefully, hoping to see what it was that he and Mr Kelly were continually working on. Not one word could I read, however, for although it was all written in Dr Dee's neat hand, it was either lists and tables of numbers, or signs and cyphers.

Packing for Dr Dee was especially trying, for as soon as we had several of his great leather-bound volumes carefully wrapped and stowed he'd discover that he needed to consult them, or wanted to change them for others. While Mistress Midge's lips moved in many a silent oath during these changes I managed to go about my duties smiling, for I was very much looking forward to being in London – especially knowing that for some little time Mistress Midge and I were going to be on our own. This, of course, would leave me more time to undertake tasks for Tomas.

I'd sewed myself a big cloth bag to keep safe my few possessions: my washing cloths, a comb, a piece of looking-glass mirror, some reddening for my cheeks and lips that Isabelle had given me and a chunk of soap and a towel. I neatly rolled my kirtles and bodices and fitted these in the bag as well, and found room also for a spare petticoat, my house slippers and a pair of high pattens to lift me above the London cobbles (for everyone said that mud and muck lay thick on London streets whether the weather was good or no).

That night, Mr Kelly stayed until very late, he and Dr Dee (I observed from my visits to the library to make up the fires) spending hours over their mathematical tables. By eleven of the clock, however, Mr Kelly went at last to his own lodgings and Dr Dee retired for the night, so I made one last call to the library to damp down the fires and make sure the candles were properly extinguished.

Both fires were still glowing slightly when I went in and there was the moon shining through the end window, so it was not entirely dark. This window was of stained glass, however, and the light it cast blue-tinted and somewhat eerie, causing me to hum a tune under my breath just to prove to myself that I wasn't afeared.

I'd brought a bucket of wet leaves with me and I

pressed a handful of these on to the first fire to dampen it down, and was about to move to the other when I heard a pattering noise, causing me to down my bucket and lift the skirts of my kirtle immediately. If there's one thing I can't abide it's mice, for I have an irrational fear of them running up between my petticoat skirts and not being able to find their way down again. The pattering turned into a different sound, however, and I stood immobile for a moment, just listening.

I might have supposed it to be something supernatural, seeing as I was in the very heart of a magician's lair. I did not, however, because I knew a secret about this room: in the large disused fireplace there was a hidey-hole which had been made for the use of Catholic priests after performing an illegal Mass. I'd found it when the girls and I had been playing hide-and-seek, and had actually hidden there myself in order to see the queen when she visited Dr Dee. It was from this direction – the old fireplace – that the sounds were coming from.

I stood very still, waiting, and after a moment a dark, stooped shape appeared in the fireplace opening. This made me fear for an instant – not that it was something supernatural – but that it might be a robber with a knife who could slit me open in a trice and make off with Dr Dee's valuable things.

Thinking this, I should have screamed and roused the household, but did not, for something told me that this person meant no harm. (Besides, if it was a robber, it was a very small one.)

I waited until the figure had emerged into the room, then, realising who it was, let out a little gasp of surprise.

The figure started back. 'Go to, Missus, you gave me a fright!'

'And you gave *me* a fright!' I retorted. 'What are you doing here?'

The small boy before me – Sonny, as Isabelle had named him – scowled at me. His coif was off and his head gleamed in the light from my candle. 'I'm here because I don't want to go back to Christ's Horspiddle. I hates it there.'

'So you followed me?'

'Nah. I saw which way you went and I asked your lady-friend what house you lived in. She told me 'twas the magician's house.'

I looked at him severely. 'And then?'

'Well, when the cart came for us to go back, I hid. No one missed me. Then I just asked about till I found me way here.' His shoulders sagged and he gave me a forlorn look, such as I'd seen beggars on the streets give. 'I thought, there's a kind gel there, one who'd give a poor boy an 'ome.'

I ignored this blatant attempt to gain my sympathy. 'But how did you get in without anyone seeing you?'

'I bunked in through the kitchen window late last night. No one saw me 'cept the monkey – and he's not telling.'

'And then what did you do?'

'Had summat to eat from the larder, then walked about the house for a bit and found this little hidey-hole. I been here all day. I went to sleep while those old coves were talking on and on.' He gestured around at the contents of the library. 'And ain't this a right queer set-up?'

I ignored this. 'You can't stay here,' I said.

'Why not? I wouldn't do nothing bad.'

'You can't set up home in a fireplace!'

He shrugged. 'Be all right. Better than at Christ's.'

'Dr Dee would be furiously angry if he found you. Besides, I'm leaving the house tomorrow so I couldn't look out for you or bring you food.'

His bottom lip quivered. 'Please, Missus. Just let's stay a little while, till I get me strength back. I just need a bit o' food and somewhere to shelter. I'll give you me sixpence if you let me bide a while.'

His voice trembled too, but I'd seen enough beggars to know play-acting when I saw it. 'You really can't,' I said firmly. 'Dr Dee isn't the sort of master who would take kindly to strangers in the house. If he found you, he'd hand you over to the magistrates and have you deported.'

'Just let me stay tonight, then,' he said. 'One single night. You wouldn't chuck a poor boy out into the freezing cold, would you, Missus? You might have a death on yer hands.'

I sighed, recalling the way that I'd used almost this

54

same ploy some months back in order to persuade Mistress Midge to let *me* stay. 'All right,' I said, 'but you must come into the kitchen and make do with an old blanket on the floor there. If Dr Dee ever found that someone had been in his library . . .'

"Course I will, Missus! I was going to the kitchen anyway to find myself a few vittles. I'll leave everything as fine as can be. No one will know I've been here!'

And so I left him in the kitchen – and was awake most of the night worried in case I'd misjudged him and that he was making away with Dr Dee's treasures.

Chapter Five

I slept in a little the following morning on account of my late night, and, making my way towards the kitchen at seven o'clock, was alarmed to discover that Mistress Midge had reached the kitchen before me. Poor Sonny, if he'd been discovered and had come up against the rough side of her temper this early in the morning!

Pushing open the kitchen door, however, I was astonished to see Sonny sitting at the table. He was wrapped in a blanket and tucking into a bowl of rabbit stew and dumplings left from the previous evening, while Mistress Midge stood by the fire, a ladle at the ready to replenish his bowl.

'Who's this, then?' I asked, raising my eyebrows at Sonny to communicate that he shouldn't speak out of turn.

'This is Sonny,' she said. 'I found him near froze to

death on the back doorstep!'

'On the *doorstep*?' I asked, startled.

'Almost gone, he was.'

Sonny looked up pathetically between mouthfuls of stew. 'I owe this fine lady my life, 'deed I do,' he croaked.

'But where does he come from?'

'From London. He was hired for a big funeral in Barnes and the cart went back without him! Imagine that.'

'Hmmm . . .' I murmured.

'So I said he could hitch a lift back to London tomorrow on our wherry. He can help us carry the books.'

Sonny managed a wan little smile. 'Be pleased to be of help as long as me strength holds up, Missus.' He wiped the back of his hand across his mouth. 'Is there a bit more bread to be had?'

I cut him a chunk of yesterday's loaf. 'Here,' I said, and couldn't resist adding, 'but are you sure you've got the strength to help us with heavy books?'

He nodded, his chin awash with grease. 'I think I'll be all right – as long as I can manage to get enough vittles down me.'

He *did* manage to get a hearty amount of food down him, and then sat toasting hunks of bread – and his feet – before the fire. When Mistress Midge went upstairs to take washing water to the mistress, I took the opportunity to ask Sonny what he'd been doing on the doorstep.

'Oh, I weren't there all night!' he said. 'I heard yon cook coming and got out on the doorstep quick. Then I made some little noises until she heard me and hauled me in. Saved me life, she did.' He added cheerfully, 'Least, that's what she thinks.'

Perhaps I should have tweaked his ear for having such cheek, but I did not.

When Merryl and Beth came to breakfast I told them that Mistress Midge had found Sonny on the doorstep. I asked them not to tell their mother or father about him, and said that I'd be taking him back to the foundlings' home as soon as we got to London.

The girls were rather delighted with him, exclaiming how grubby and tiny he was (for he was as scrawny as a day-old rabbit despite the amount of food he was capable of putting away). They admired his shiny scalp, all the more so when he told them that it was shaved every week to keep the lice off, and, discovering he could do tricks with cards and coins, they fell to treating him much as they did their pet monkey, carrying him from chair to stool and making him their baby. He took all this in good part, for I believe it was the first time he'd ever been made such a fuss of, and the three children plus the real monkey entertained each other most of that day, leaving me and Mistress Midge to get on with the packing and stacking of boxes ready to be taken to London. There was a great deal to see to, Dr

Dee having ordered that we should take as much as possible in the wherry with us.

I found time to say goodbye to Isabelle that day and because I knew I'd be seeing Merryl and Beth very soon, my only regret on leaving Mortlake was that my ma wouldn't know where I was. When last I'd seen her, I'd assured her that in the event of any emergency, I could be found in Mortlake, at the magician's house, and anyone locally would be able to tell her where this was. Supposing, I thought now, one of my sisters was poorly and Ma needed to tell me of it – or suppose she was sick herself and no one knew how to reach me? I pondered on this problem for some time but found no solution to it, for even if I'd been able to obtain parchment to send her my new address I had no money to pay for a messenger to go as far as Hazelgrove. Besides – and this decided it – neither Ma nor my sisters could read.

I thought about my family and of home as I packed boxes, tied up books and wrapped utensils, musing on the last day I'd spent there: the day of the village Michelmas Fair. On this day the great lady of our manor, the splendidly gowned and jewelled Lady Margaret Ashe (who had, in her youth, been lady-in-waiting to our queen) had opened the fair and entreated us all to enjoy ourselves. I'd been doing just that when my father had come along with his threats and his bullying, causing me to run away.

But perhaps I had reason to be grateful to him, I

thought, for if he'd not been such a bully and a tyrant then I might never have landed up in the magician's house and so met Tomas.

We had to catch the morning tide, and Old Jake, who was sometimes employed by Dr Dee to do odd jobs around the place, arrived with a cart early the next morning to take everything down to the wharf. Mistress Midge and I were ready for him and, having been up since an icy-cold five of the clock, surrounded and befuddled by all the pots, pans, boxes and bundles we had to take with us, were pleased to be on the move at last.

Sonny was a little quiet; probably because we'd explained to him that as soon as we arrived in London he'd have to be taken back to Christ's Hospital. Our neighbour, Mistress Gove, had assured us that it was against the law to steal a child from a foundlings' home, and that we could be punished for doing so. Informing Sonny of this, I'd told him several times that he'd be better off in a permanent place, that at least they'd see he was always fed and sheltered – and in time they'd apprentice him to a shoemaker or baker so that he had a good trade. Whenever I started on this all too familiar track, however, he'd taken to putting his hands over his ears and whistling so that he couldn't hear me.

The journey was not pleasant, for an icy wind swept up the river and sleet fell, making the three of us retreat into a little wooden cabin at the fore of the boat. I'd hoped to see lots of important buildings along the way, but most of the time it was just too wet and dreary for me to put my head out of the cabin.

When, in the afternoon, the weather improved and I looked out, we'd almost reached London and everything seemed to appear at once: Lambeth Palace went by at the same time as another most wonderful church on the opposite bank; then came towering warehouses with strange and wonderful contraptions called cranes standing alongside landing stages; after that, spacious houses with gardens containing neatly clipped trees of box and bay all in rows, and here and there knot gardens like the queen's privy garden at Richmond. There was a deal here to look at, for the river traffic increased greatly as we neared London and many other wherries, tilt boats, small craft with sails, ferry boats and barges appeared. Most of the barges carried coal, timber or waste, but one was beautiful and gilded (putting me in mind of the royal barge that Her Grace used to travel the river between palaces), and Sonny said this was sure to belong to one of the livery companies. Between all these craft, lines of icy-white swans glided about looking for food, seemingly unconscious of all the activity around them.

We began to smell London at this stage: the same stench which swept upriver to Mortlake when the wind blew from that direction, but though Mistress Midge began complaining and holding her nose, to me this odious smell didn't seem much to bear when you thought of all the other delights the city offered.

Seeing other watermen, our two rowers began to name-call and trade insults and profanities with them, which surprised us very much. Sonny, red-faced and giggling fit to bust at their words, explained that watermen had reputations as the foulest-speaking and most blasphemous men in London, and indeed I heard that day many amazing and ingenious insults which I stored away until such time as I might have a use for them.

We passed the riverside walls of Whitehall Palace and I could not contain my wonder at this mighty building, for it was beyond large, seeming to be the size of a small town. Going past more buildings, a prison, a church and some magnificent houses with lavish front gardens running down to the river, we at last reached Puddle Dock. There were several fellows waiting here with hand-carts for hire, and Mistress Midge selected one of these and asked the man to load all the baggage and boxes on to his cart and convey us to the house Dr Dee had rented, which we'd been told was on the corner of Milk Street and Green Lane.

Mistress Midge is a slow walker, so it took us some time to get to this address. Here we received a welcome of sorts when a window in the house next door flew open and a bowl of dirty water was thrown out with the cry 'Mind yerselves below!'

'This is never it!' said Mistress Midge, staring up at the house and brushing drops of water from her skirts.

'This is the corner of Milk Street and Green Lane, lady,' said the carter, and he began to take our things off the cart at some speed, for I suppose he wanted to get back to the wharf for another hiring.

Mistress Midge and I stood outside, looking up at the house before us. It seemed to lean sideways, its window frames sloping this way and giving it a drunken appearance. Two windows were broken and had been repaired with brown paper, and it seemed that all the woodwork, frames and beams had once been painted green, but these were now blistered and peeling.

'Lord above!' Mistress Midge sighed. 'The mistress won't like this.'

'No, indeed,' I said.

'I don't like the look of it myself, for it seems a nasty, mean sort of place and 'tis probably running with rats.' She suddenly seemed to notice that the carter was placing boxes all across the door, inhibiting our entry. 'Not there, you rapscallion!' she roared. 'Weren't you born with any sense? How are we supposed to get in?'

Whistling, careless, he removed the boxes and Mistress Midge produced a key which opened the front door. Inside we found a dusty, cobwebby hall. This gave way to rooms which, although fair-sized, were piled high with empty crates, husks of corn and rotting cabbages. These stank abysmally, causing us both to hold our noses. My heart sank. It was a long way from how I'd envisaged living in London.

'Dr Dee told me that the house had once been home to a family who bought and sold vegetables,' Mistress Midge said. She nodded sagely. 'And here's what they did with those stuffs they couldn't sell ...'

There were smaller rooms at the back of the house, one of these a kitchen with a range, oven and turning spit. Outside was a courtyard shared between the row of houses, a soakaway for the emptying of chamber pots, a well and a privy to be shared with the neighbours. In all the rooms, upstairs and down, broken furniture, gnarled, stinking vegetables or rubbish lay on the floor. The walls were so damp that mildew and fungi grew on them and the windows, if not broken, were grimy. To top it all the husky smell of mouse hung in the air.

Mistress Midge observed these rooms, taking a horrified breath in each until finally she was as puffed up as a pigeon.

'Good God alive!' she finally exploded. 'What are we supposed to do with this filthy piggery? Does he really think we can turn this hole into a place a lady would want to live? What if Her Grace came to visit, as she did in Mortlake?'

'Perhaps we won't find it so bad once we start work,' I said lamely.

'Not so bad! It'll be worse, you mark my words! This is a rat hole, a kennel, a fly-bitten pigsty of a place!'

Shouting and muttering by turn, she paid the carter and then the three of us set about clearing the fireplace so that we could light a fire and warm ourselves. At least we could do that, I thought, for there was rubbish aplenty to burn. And in the morning, perhaps, things would look better.

Chapter Six

Of course, things did not look better, for the day dawned mild and clear and the bright morning sunshine streaming into the rooms showed up the squalor even more. The three of us spent several hours clearing two rooms, piling up the few things that were worth saving (a chair, an oak chest, some bedsteads with old straw mattresses and a few blankets) and putting all the rest of the rubbish in the yard at the back ready to burn. Sonny worked very hard, for of course he was hoping to make himself so invaluable to us that we'd keep him. Come the afternoon, however (finding Mistress Midge's continual muttering and grousing most wearying), I offered to go out for provisions and take Sonny back to Christ's Hospital at the same time.

'Oh, no, Missus!' he cried, looking very anguished.

I shot him a sympathetic smile, for I own I felt sorry

for the little lad. I wished that he didn't have to be returned, but Mistress Gove's words had hit hard and we were uneasy in our minds about having him there if it meant we were to fall foul of the law.

We tidied him as best we could and, though he would not suffer his face to be washed, I brushed off an amount of dust that had accumulated on his black funeral clothes and made him polish his shoes. Before we set off he had a large wedge of pie that had been left over from our tavern meal of the night before, and Mistress Midge also wrapped up a large piece of cheese for him to take.

Asked where the foundlings' home was situated, Sonny answered in a gloomy voice that it was at the old Greyfriars Monastery in Newgate Street. 'But if you take me back I'll only run away again,' he added.

'And where would you be, then?' I asked. 'Out on the streets with no shelter and no one to feed you.'

'I'd fend for meself all right. I'd hold horses for gents or card wool. I'd beg on the streets if I had to.'

'If you did that the watchmen would catch you and take you to the workhouse as a vagrant.'

'Don't care,' he said. 'I hates Christ's Horspiddle.'

I squeezed his hand. He wouldn't want to be seen holding hands with me, but I couldn't trust him not to run off. 'Perhaps you'll like it a little better there now, after some time away.'

'I shall like it worse!' he retorted.

'But you must have friends there. What about the

other boys?'

He looked up at me balefully. 'No family. No friends. 'Tis every boy for hisself there and the Devil take the lad who doesn't watch his back.'

I was dismayed at this, but tried not to show it. 'You'll get on all right as time goes on,' I said encouragingly. ''Tis a sight better than sleeping on Thames mud – and in a few years you can go to be a grocer or a wheelwright and will be running rowdy with the other 'prentices.'

He didn't reply and I didn't prolong this line of reasoning any longer, I'm ashamed to say, because I was so rapt at the scenes of London life unfolding before me: at the horse-riders with their silver stirrups jangling, the busy shops, the painted carriages, the hackney coaches and grand ladies being carried aloft in curtained litters. Other well-dressed and highly perfumed ladies walked, I noticed, but were flanked front and back by footmen carrying fur blankets against the cold, and spare shoes and gloves in case milady should fall foul of the mud. And, of course, there *was* mud and filth running down channels in the centre of the lanes, and beggars all in rags and sacking, and children without shoes shaking with cold, but that day, my first in London, I hardly saw these poor creatures at all, for I was so bewitched by everything else.

Coming to a crossroads, an ancient tavern named the George caught my eye. It was built in an L-shape with two long galleries overlooking a courtyard, and people were standing along these looking down upon a story being enacted on the platform below. Everyone seemed to be enjoying it, for there was much laughter and shouts of acclaim from the onlookers.

My first thought was that it might be a masque with jesters (and of course my mind went to Tomas), but then I saw a board written with the words *The Queen's Players* and the name of the performance, which was *The Two Gentlemen of Verona*.

Sonny and I stood watching for some moments at the entrance to the courtyard and I realised that it was not a masque that was being performed – for I'd seen these played at Court over Christmas, and they'd had persons representing Spring and Autumn and Love and so on – but a merry story acted out as if in real life. There was applause and whistling from the audience, especially when a pretty girl (whom I own must have been a very comely man) came on to the stage and showed the audience a dainty turn of ankle.

'Shall we go nearer to see a little more?' I asked Sonny.

He looked at me and shook his head, frowning. ''Tis not for the likes of ladies such as you.'

'I'm hardly that!'

'But playhouses are where the nightwalkers go to find their customers.'

I laughed, surprised that he even knew what the word 'nightwalker' meant. 'Surely not?'

''Tis true! I've heard the bigger boys talking about it,

69

telling of how much it costs.' He pulled at my hand, embarrassed. 'Indeed you cannot go in there, Missus.'

I studied the audience, both on the balconies and those standing around the players at ground level. Possibly what Sonny said was true, for there were very few females around – and while those on the balconies may have been of a more refined appearance, those downstairs seemed to be wearing very frivolous head-dresses and showing a substantial amount of bosom.

'You may be right,' I said, 'but nevertheless it looks a great deal of fun and I shall come back another time and watch. If I do, I shall dress discreetly and conceal myself behind the largest gentleman I can find,' I assured him.

We went on towards Christ's Hospital, and with every step Sonny's feet trudged ever more slowly and his head drooped further on to his chest, so that I had to remind myself continually that he was a professional mourner and had been trained to turn the melancholy on and off as simply as one could turn a handle. As we neared Newgate, I began to see some young boys wear-ing long, heavy, blue cassocks shaped with gathered skirts such as a parson might wear, together with bright-yellow woollen stockings. I asked Sonny what these signified and he, sighing, told me that this was the uniform for Christ's Hospital and he would be required to put his on as soon as he arrived back.

'It looks very smart,' I assured him.

'D'you think so? The yellow is to keep the rats from

biting us – for they don't like the colour – and the blue coats are to mark us out from the rest of society and are monstrous hot in summer. D'you see those white bands about the boys' necks?'

I nodded.

'They must stay white at all times. If we are seen with one spot o' dirt on them, we get a beating.'

I changed the subject, telling Sonny that Mistress Midge and I would visit him and bring him food.

'Ah, but you won't be living in London long, will you, Missus?' was his response. 'And what will I do after that?'

'But you *are* fed regularly there.'

He nodded. 'Black bread three times a day. Meat once a week if we're lucky.'

I had no way of knowing if he was telling the truth, but assured him again that, while we stayed in London, Mistress Midge or I would bring him food whenever we were able.

The old Greyfriars Monastery was an imposing place and Sonny, usually so cheery and self-possessed, shrank against me as we walked into the quadrangle. I explained to a man wearing the same blue uniform that I was returning a lost boy and was directed to the grammar master's office. Crossing an expanse of muddy grass to reach this, I looked through a window and saw rows of boys kneeling in prayer, all wearing the same identical yellow socks and blue cassocks (for which reason Mistress Midge told me later they were sometimes called the Bluecoat Boys). From the grammar master we were shown to Matron's room, and then on to the bursar. He was a fierce and angry sort of man, who, seeming to take me for some sort of orphan as well, roared at me to take Sonny to the boys' dormitory and then to go to the girls' workhouse.

I couldn't help but be a little horrified at all this, for I'd told myself that there would be at least one person pleased to see Sonny back – to welcome him into the fold – but if there was, I'd not found them. Moreover, it seemed that no one even knew nor cared that he'd been missing. Perhaps Mistress Gove had been wrong.

'What did you think, then, Missus?' Sonny said when I mentioned my puzzlement. 'There are more than four hundred boys here. Who is there to mark *my* absence? No one cares a jot whether I live or die.'

I suddenly thought of my own ma and her sorrow when we'd parted, and could not reply straight away because of the lump in my throat. 'Someone cared enough to name you well,' I said when I could speak. 'For Sonny is a good and merry name. And Sonny Day is even better,' I added, for he'd told us that this was what he was known as at the Hospital.

'Do you think so, Missus?' Sonny blew out his cheeks in derision. 'I was named so because when I was dumped outside the gates it was a sunny day. And others are named according to where they're found.'

'What are you saying?' I asked, puzzled.

'Just this, one boy's called James Storm because he

was chucked out in wet weather. Another's called Peter Back-stairs. Another is John Doorway.'

I looked at him in dismay.

'We are waiting for a boy to be abandoned in the privies,' he said, at which statement I did not know whether to laugh or cry.

The boys' dormitory was up a twisting stone staircase which grew steeper the higher we went, and at the top opened out into a long alleyway of beds stretching the whole length of the building. The beds were narrow with wooden sides, so that they looked like small coffins. They were a regulation distance from each other, and each had a layer of straw and a neatly folded grey blanket at the bottom. There was just space enough for an upturned wooden crate between each bed and these, I could see, held the boys' clothes.

'Which is your bed?' I asked. 'You had better change into your blue coat.'

He scratched his head. 'I sleeps somewhere 'ere,' he said, his brow creasing as he walked along the line. 'I bunks in with a bigger boy; we tops and tails it. Though he always gets the blanket,' he added. He sat himself down on a bed. 'This is the one.'

'Very well, but if he hogs the blanket then you must ask whoever is in charge of you for another. One of your own,' I said, but he gave me such a scornful look that I knew I'd said something absurd.

Looking round then, the empty room faded away and I had a sudden vision of the dormitory at night:

poorly lit by tallow tapers, the boys lying in their allotted spaces two to a bed. I saw they were of all ages: near-babes sharing some bunks, full-grown boys of twelve in others. Sonny, blanket-less, was staring up at the ceiling, arms around himself to keep warm. I saw a stoutly built boy, a V-shaped scar on one cheek, kicking out at Sonny's bed, then bending forwards, pulling at Sonny's ears and then pinching him hard on both cheeks so that he cried out and sat up. The boy pulled Sonny to his feet by the neck of his nightshirt, then slapped him – and at this point I shook my head to drive the vision away, because I couldn't bear to see any more.

I heard myself saying to Sonny, 'Don't bother to change back into your blue coat. You're not stopping.'

'*What?*'

'We're going back to Green Lane. You don't have to stop here.'

He looked across the coffin-beds at me, half bewildered, half hopeful. 'D'you really mean it, Missus?'

I nodded, holding out my hand. 'No one seems bothered whether you're here or not, so you might as well come back with me.'

He hesitated a moment. 'Will it be all right?' he breathed. 'Won't you get 'rested by the constable?'

'I shouldn't think so,' I said.

'An' what about yon cook?'

'I'll sort it out with her . . .'

No one stopped us going out of the place, no one called after us, so we just kept on walking the quickest way home. On the way I asked Sonny how the bigger boys treated the younger ones, if they'd been nice to him, and was treated to another of his scornful looks.

'Was there anyone in particular you didn't like?' I asked.

'I should say. There was a stout cove we named Big Billie, who had a scar on his face he said he got from fighting a wolf.' Sonny drew a finger down and up his cheek in a 'V' motion. 'He used to come round the lads' beds at night and if they had anything good he'd shake it out of 'em.'

I nodded. Strangely, it was just as I'd visualised.

Reaching the house, I told Sonny to hide himself in the hall cupboard while I found the right moment to talk nicely to Mistress Midge. As it happened, though, I didn't have to say anything at all, for on seeing me she put down her broom and turned to me, her plump face creased with concern.

'I've been thinking about that lad,' she said. 'It can't be much of a life for him in that place – that foundlings' home.'

I shook my head. 'No, I don't suppose it is.'

'What was it like? A dirty hole, I'll be bound.'

'It wasn't dirty,' I said, 'for the boys have to keep it clean and Lord help them if they don't. It was just sad and lonely.'

'Ah,' she said, shaking her head and sighing. 'But did he settle in all right? Had anyone been asking for him?'

I shook my head. 'I don't think so. There are near four hundred boys there and he said he didn't have a friend amongst them.'

She gave a sharp cry. 'I knew it! You never should have taken him back.' She glared at me accusingly. 'Why ever did you do such a thing?'

'I thought we agreed . . . because of what Mistress Gove said.'

'Pah! Who is she to tell us? Just because her daughter is married to a nightwatchman she thinks she knows the law.'

'Do you wish he hadn't gone back, then?' I asked. 'Do you wish we'd have kept him here with us?'

'Indeed I do,' she said stoutly.

'But what would we have done with him when the Dee family arrived?'

She frowned, then her face cleared. 'Told Dr Dee, and kept him on as a boot boy.'

'But what if the parish constable should have come a-calling?'

'Psshh! We could have disguised the lad, grown his hair . . . dressed him in Merryl's clothes and pretended he was a girl!'

There was a scuffle as Sonny burst out of the hall cupboard. 'No, Missus! I won't wear lace petticoats, indeed I won't!'

Mistress Midge gaped at me. 'What . . . ?'

'I couldn't leave him,' I said. We both turned to stare at Sonny. 'He seemed so small and helpless, and had no one to speak for him.'

We turned to face Sonny, who was no doubt torn between appearing helpless and wanting to assume his customary grin and swagger. 'I like it here better, Missus,' he said. 'You gets more vittles.'

Chapter Seven

A week later, although the house had been cleared of rubbish and was swept clean, it was not yet suitable to be lived in by members of polite society. Mistress Midge said in view of *she who might visit*, it was essential that it reached a certain level of comfort and refinement, but the walls of the rooms were mouldy with damp, and the whole house needed a coat of paint and two coats of distemper. As for the furniture – well, the old mattresses were good enough for Mistress Midge and me, and Sonny always slept in the kitchen in front of the fire – but for the Dee family, new mattresses and bedsteads would have to be purchased, as well as certain other items.

Mistress Midge proposed that we should inform Dr Dee of all this and ask for his instructions, and accordingly I purchased a sheet of parchment, a quill and some ink to write to him. As I wrote (and this took some considerable time and much chewing of the end of the quill) I was aware that I was giving away a secret, for until then I'd kept him ignorant of the fact that I could read and write. The letter completed, however, I added my loving wishes to Beth and Merryl and said I hoped they were doing well at their studies, for they would have restarted lessons with their tutor.

We decided we should let Sonny take the letter back to Mortlake, for this seemed an ideal opportunity to show how useful he was, and Mistress Midge asked me to add a few lines saying that Sonny was being of considerable help and suggesting, if Dr Dee approved, that he stay on as a go-between ready to travel between the two households. We'd already been to a rag fair and exchanged Sonny's black crêpe funeral clothes (which were a very decent quality) for two pairs of breeches and a jacket, and Mistress Midge had also purchased a cap to hide his shaven head. Early in the morning, therefore, the letter set securely inside his jacket, Sonny set off for the river steps, intending to take a place on one of the barges going upriver to Mortlake and pay his way by helping load and unload whatever goods they were carrying.

As we said goodbye to him at the front door my eyes stung a little, for I'd become attached to him in the time he'd been with us, and he seemed very young to be undertaking such journeys up and down the river.

'Do you think he'll return?' Mistress Midge asked as we waved him off.

'Of course!'

'You don't think he'll just make a bolt for freedom?'

I shook my head. 'I think not. All he wants is to live with a family and be fed at regular intervals.'

Having been busy since we'd arrived, sweeping, scrubbing, washing down walls and cleaning windows, I'd hardly had a spare moment to think about Tomas. Now that the house was reasonably clean, however, and Mistress Midge and I had little to do until Sonny returned with Dr Dee's instructions, I turned my thoughts to Whitehall and those within it, wondering if Tomas knew I'd arrived (surely he did, if he was any sort of a spy?) and how long it would be before he contacted me. I wondered, too, about the new lady-in-waiting and whether she'd settled into her position at Court. I found myself hoping that she had not; that she had been quite dreadfully homesick and had had to return to wherever she'd come from.

It didn't often happen that servants found themselves with time on their hands, and while I wasted mine thinking about Tomas, Mistress Midge turned to more practical matters and profited by it. There being an ancient oven, she took the opportunity to try out a recipe her sister had given her: a seasonal treat consisting of gingerbread cut into an oval – roughly a mouse's shape – and glazed with a little melted white sugar and egg white. These mice, with a currant nose and string tail, proved to be extremely popular with our neighbours on each side and beyond, and Mistress Midge decided she'd make a batch every day and sell them at the door. She knew, of course, that this activity would have to cease as soon as the Dee family arrived, but until then she was going to earn some money to put aside for her old age.

For two mornings I contented myself by helping her glaze the mice and give them currant noses, then realised that I was wasting valuable time. I was in London; surely I could find myself a more exciting pastime? The next thought came hot along on the heels of the first: I would attend a play at the George Inn . . .

I told Mistress Midge what I intended and to my surprise she was as shocked as Sonny had been. 'You certainly cannot go to a play,' she cried. 'They're for horse thieves, rich men and their painted strumpets!'

'That's a monstrous old-fashioned view,' I objected, conveniently forgetting the array of scantily dressed women I'd seen before. 'The queen goes to plays now. The Court go. There's a theatre company named the Queen's Players. Would Her Grace allow her name to be employed if there was anything in the least bit indecent about attending a performance?'

Mistress Midge paused in the act of lifting a tray of newly cooked gingerbread mice out of the oven. 'Even so, what holds for the Court does not hold for the rest of the world, for *they* have special rules. I'm telling you that no decent woman would be seen playgoing.'

I sniffed, enjoying the gingery-sweet smell on the air.

'Once 'twas known that you'd been in the audience you'd be labelled as a woman of easy virtue.'

'But no one about here knows me.'

'What about our new neighbours?' she said, meaning those in Green Lane who'd been buying her sugared mice.

'If they're at the inn to see me, then they're as guilty of loose living as I am. Which, as you know, is not at all,' I added.

She shook her head, frowning. 'You risk losing your reputation and being the object of unwanted attentions. Take my advice: if you go to such a place, then go in a man's garb.'

I was about to laugh at this notion, then stopped and thought about it. Whether she was right or not about playgoing, I didn't want to be the subject of any man's attentions. Perhaps going dressed as one was the sensible thing to do . . .

Between us, Mistress Midge and I improvised a costume. She owned a white shirt which gathered into a small ruff at the neck (and having no other decoration, was suitable apparel for either sex) and I found I could just get into Sonny's spare pair of breeches. I had some dark, newly darned hose and stout footwear and wore a short jacket of my own which fastened with plain wooden pegs. I tugged my hair off my face and fastened it on top of my head so that it lay as flat as possible, and over it wore the black, close-fitting coif that Sonny had worn as a funeral mute.

This concealed every bit of hair (although, I own, was none too attractive).

I dressed, then went to the kitchen, where Mistress Midge, busily glazing her mice, looked me up and down and laughed heartily. 'You make a fine youth,' she declared, 'if a little on the short side. What will your name be?'

'Why? I don't intend to introduce myself to anyone!'

'Nevertheless, you must have a name ready in case you're asked. And an occupation.'

'Surely not . . .'

'And you mustn't trill or giggle, but develop a manly guffaw for the vulgar parts of the play. There will be many of those,' she added darkly. She bowed to me. 'And your name, young man, is . . . ?'

'Is . . . is Luke!'

'And what do you do, young Luke?'

'I'm a glove-maker and embroiderer,' I said, giving my old occupation.

Mistress Midge shook her head. 'You must have a more manly job.'

'I'm training to be a cook in an important house-hold.'

'That's better.' She nodded slowly. 'And yes, 'tis plausible that, after helping serve dinner at midday, you might be allowed out of the house on occasion for a play's two o'clock performance.'

I gave a flourish of my hand and bowed from the waist, as I'd seen Tomas bow to the queen – although I could not, of course, doff my hat.

Mistress Midge beamed. 'It's years since I had such attentions from a fine young man,' she said, then stood back and studied me. 'You need a little beard, perhaps . . .'

'Never!' I said in alarm.

'Just some shading around your jaw . . .' She bent over the fire and, taking a little coal dust, brushed it over my chin. 'There,' she said, 'a suggestion of a beard is all that's needed. It gives you a certain dignity.'

'I'm playgoing,' I reminded her, 'not taking service at St Dominic's.' But I let the stubbled look remain, to please her.

I enjoyed my stroll to the George. At first I was unsure of how to conduct myself and felt awkward and self-conscious, but, seeing a group of youths, fell in behind them and began to imitate their swagger. Copying them, I kept my head high and if anyone stared at me, looked back boldly instead of lowering my glance. I found it refreshing to take large strides instead of small and dainty ones, to be wearing breeches instead of a kirtle and petticoats, which had to be constantly lifted out of the mud, and to have my hair tucked away and not blowing itself into tangles. Most of all I enjoyed not being the object of the 'prentices' attentions, for in London they were much cheekier than those at Mortlake, and would catcall and whistle whenever a girl passed.

Reaching the inn, I paid my penny as a groundling and found myself a space to stand in the courtyard. There were seats to be had along the balconies at a greater expense, and also some downstairs, though the ones actually on the stage cost sixpence. Paying this amount meant you were very close to the action, and – as I soon saw – could join the actors on stage for a crowd scene or (as frequently happened) interrupt the play in order to give the audience the benefit of your wit and opinions. The actors did not seem to mind this in the least and, when the interval came, returned the favour by stepping down and mingling with the richer members of the audience.

The audience was very mixed. There were some extremely well-dressed gentlemen in the best seats wearing plush velvet and plumed hats, and a few ladies scattered amongst these. I gave the females careful inspection in order to report back to Mistress Midge, and indeed they *did* seem to be very loud. They had pronounced London accents and were wearing low-cut dresses in violent shades which exposed a considerable amount of bosom. (This was nothing new to me, however, for the ladies at Court, though they spoke in low and cultured voices, were often gowned in a similarly revealing manner.) It was difficult to see if their faces were painted, for almost without exception these were concealed behind elaborate fans, or they wore masks held up by means of a button clenched between their front teeth.

The play was the same one as before, *The Two Gentlemen of Verona*, and was advertised as being written by one who was a player as well as a playwright, a Mr William Shakespeare. I cannot say whether it was good or not, however, for the audience around me both on and off the stage was so boisterous that I kept losing the sense of the plot. I did discern that it was about two young men who are best friends, and one of them goes travelling while the other stays with his sweetheart, and afterwards they fall in love with different ladies . . . but then the whole play became a muddle to me. There were some funny speeches and also much bawdiness, causing me to admit to Mistress Midge after that, if I'd been there as my real self, I might have blushed and hung my head for shame at the words used. Seeing as I was a young man named Luke, however, I did not, but instead slapped my thigh and laughed as loudly as everyone else.

The play ended with enemies being reconciled and lovers reunited, and as a fiddler struck up and the audience began to leave, two men stationed themselves on each side of the courtyard to give out bills advertising the next play in their repertoire.

I pushed through the crowd, who, seemingly reluctant to leave, were gathered in little groups, posturing and declaiming, and took a leaflet. It was for a performance the following week of a new play named *The Country Husband*, in a building specially constructed for such a purpose and named the Curtain.

Reading the bill, I thought I'd certainly like to go to such a place – and as long as Dr Dee and his family took their time getting to London, then there was no reason why I shouldn't.

'Hey, boy!' someone shouted above the crowd, but, not used to being addressed this way, I didn't take any notice.

'You in the old man's cap!'

I looked around then, knowing it was probably me who was being addressed.

The speaker was one of the two men standing in the doorway; the man who'd handed me the leaflet. He was tall, with a barrel stomach, a gingery cloud of a beard and one gold earring (which I'd noticed before was the fashion in London).

'Yes, you. Come back here, will you?' he beckoned.

I pulled myself up to my full height, which is not so very great, and went to him, trying to look uncon-cerned. It was not against the law to feign being a man, surely? 'Do you want something?' I asked gruffly.

'I saw you looking at the playbill.'

I was puzzled at this. 'Yes?'

'You can read?'

I nodded.

'Could you read and learn a few words?'

I shrugged. 'Of course. If I had to.'

He looked me up and down and nodded approval. 'I must tell you,' he said, 'that youths like you are much sought after.'

I was a little shocked at this and immediately thought of disappearing into the crowd and getting away. I think he knew how my mind was going, however, because he held up his hand and shook his head.

'Nay,' he said, 'don't think the worst!'

I blinked at him.

'What I mean is, you are young, and of a girl's stature. Now you're close I see your features are delicate, and your voice as light as a damsel's.'

Rather alarmed, I cleared my throat and prepared to speak more deeply.

''Tis no crime if a youth's voice remains high!' he said. 'Indeed, 'tis what every actor yearns for: a girl's shape and temperament, and a soft and well-modulated voice. With these, a young man may play many parts: a dissembling coxcomb in the morning and a duchess at noon.' He smiled and bowed. 'What's your name, boy?'

'Luke, Sir,' I answered.

'Well, Luke, would you be free one afternoon to help out a band of players?'

'Perhaps . . .' I replied wonderingly.

''Tis like this, young Luke. One of our prettier players – a boy who usually acts the part of a woman – has been taken ill. Not with plague!' he put in quickly. 'But with some sort of ague, which has caused him to sweat and groan and take to his bed.'

'I see,' I said slowly.

'We have a play to perform the day after tomorrow, and no one to play his part. It's to act a maidservant –

not a large role. Do you think you could be such a person, sweeping and cleaning and so on?'

'I'm not sure . . .'

'Come, boy, 'tis not difficult! Why, if women can do it, then surely we are able.'

I hid a smile. 'Perhaps I could.'

'And could you act the female . . . be a little winsome and shy, a little modest?'

'Possibly . . .'

'You'd have a fair wig of hair on your head, of course, and a gown.' He smiled at me. 'I think with some paint on your lips, some curls and a feathered bonnet you'd make quite a passable lady.'

'I thank you, Sir,' I said, fighting down the urge to laugh. 'Though I hardly know if you have paid me a compliment or no.'

'Do it, and you'll have a free ticket to all of our performances for the rest of the season – and acting work when you want it. What do you say, boy?'

I was very excited but strove to hide it; to act more manly and considered in my reaction to his proposal. 'I think,' I paused, 'I think I shall say yes, Sir.'

'Well said!' He clapped me on the shoulder. 'And to show you are of good intent, perhaps you wouldn't mind distributing some of these bills to advertise our company's new play.' And so saying, he dumped a pile of the bills into my arms. 'No hurry with these! But come to the Curtain in Shoreditch the day after tomorrow and ask for Mr Richard James.'

'I shall, Sir!' I said, and, fearful excited and clutching the bills, broke into a run in order to get home and acquaint Mistress Midge with what had happened.

And then I stopped. No! I wouldn't go straight home. I'd go to the place I'd been longing to visit: to Whitehall Palace in my disguise, and see who I could see...

Chapter Eight

'*The Country Husband!*' I called as deep and manfully as I could. 'A new play by the Queen's Players!'

People crossing the square, which was circled by the myriad houses, shops, chapels, courts of law and apartments belonging to the Palace of Whitehall, hardly glanced at me, for I was surrounded by street folk crying the merits of their goods, as well as those there merely in the hopes of seeing the queen.

I didn't mind that no one was taking notice of me, because that gave me the opportunity to observe all the comings and goings: the horses, carriages, carts and conveyances travelling to and fro on Court business, mingling with the various members of the working population of London. I saw almost all trades represented: sweeps with long brushes over their shoulders, clergymen, farmers, bakers with trays of pastries, musicians carrying lutes, liveried coachmen, valets, gentlemen-at-arms with their pikestaffs, and all manner of women, from frowsy-looking charwomen to those dressed beautifully enough to be ladies-in-waiting to the queen. Thinking this, I touched the groat at my neck, that battered coin I wore. Had she begun to recover from having her heart broken? Might I possibly see her going about her queenly business? What was the latest news on Mary, the Scottish queen who sought to take her throne?

Occasionally someone would take a playbill from me, and I'd acknowledge my thanks with a nod of the head and a bow (which, in truth, was a lot easier than a curtsey). Observing, marvelling at all before me, I traversed the square, went under a gateway and found myself in a vast courtyard containing, in one corner, a stable block. Here could be seen scores of horses. Some of these were being groomed, some exercised, and some were just standing patiently gazing out of their open stable doors. Opposite this line of stables was an orchard, and beyond this the entrance to a tilt yard with tall stands and coloured pennants flying. People came and went busily between all of these places.

'A new play by the Queen's Players!' I called, and a young serving girl carrying a pile of starched linen napkins took a copy of my bill. She hardly glanced at it, however, and I doubted that she could read it.

'A new play!' she exclaimed. 'And are you one who acts in it?'

I cleared my throat. I'd not thought I'd have to answer any questions and I'd only rehearsed calling the same two sentences in my new, deep voice. 'Yes, I have . . . er . . . a small part to play in it,' I answered gruffly.

'Indeed!' the girl said. 'I've long wanted to go to a play. Tell me, would it be seemly for a maid to go on her own?'

This question put me in a dilemma. 'Some say it is . . .'

She smiled at me. 'And what do *you* say, master actor?'

'I say . . . perhaps it would be better if someone could accompany you. Do you not have a sweetheart?'

She lowered her head and looked at me from under her lashes. 'I do not.'

This look, and this answer, perplexed me. I'd gazed at several young men in this way, but had never before been on the receiving end of such a look and found it disconcerting. 'It may be . . . er . . . more seemly for you to go with one of the male sex.'

'But I do not have a sweetheart.' She gave a little sigh. 'And I have no time to find one, for I work in Her Majesty's laundries near every day of the year.'

'That's a pity,' I said, speaking gruff and awkward.

She smiled. 'But I sometimes get two hours off in the afternoon, so I could easily come to the playhouse! I may come and see you.'

'You may not recognise me,' I said quickly. 'I act as a girl, you see, and am to play the part of a waiting-woman.'

She laughed. 'To do that must feel very strange.'

'Not that strange,' I said before I could stop myself.

She looked at me quizzically.

'For an actor!' I added quickly. 'We are used to taking all parts: old, young, king, queen . . . ghost!'

'And for how long have you been an actor?'

'I admit, not very long,' I said truthfully, for it was less than one hour.

As we were speaking, those who looked after the horses were coming and going, and there was much noise from a nearby wooden building (which I found out later contained courts on which was played a game called tennis). Although all seemed perfectly open and informal, I could see that inside the palace doorways a guard with a sharpened halberd was standing, and if any strangers tried to force their way in, no doubt this would be used against them.

'My name is Barbara,' the girl said. She looked at me, head on one side. 'And your name, master actor?'

'My name's Luke,' I said.

'And if I should come to the theatre next week, might I see you there?'

I coughed, embarrassed. 'Perhaps, perhaps . . .' I said, raising a hand in farewell.

The girl, smiling at me all the while, carried on towards one of the nearby buildings with her pile of linens, and a group of kitchen 'prentices came up to me and asked for a bill, saying that they couldn't read but would show it to one of the cooks, who'd once said that he'd take them to a play. I told them the names of the play and theatre and had begun to walk on towards where I could see a very large and flourishing kitchen garden, when a small party of horse-riders came across the orchard, calling to each other and laughing. I looked at them and my breath caught in my throat, for as the two leading riders neared us, I saw they were no other than Tomas and the new lady-in-waiting.

My heart was thumping, but I steeled myself not to run. It would be thrilling to see Tomas again, and even more so to see how he behaved in his everyday life. Even, perhaps, discern how it stood between him and the lady, who was of course fixed in my head as my rival. I walked back towards the shadow of the stable block, pulling my coif well down my forehead and ensuring that it covered as much of my face as possible. I'd just had a maidservant flirt with me, so thought I must make a passable-looking lad. Besides, I knew from experience that the nobility hardly looked at the vast army of servants who underpinned their day-to-day lives.

I turned slightly away from the riders. 'New play at the Curtain!' I called as two street-sellers, possibly having seen potential customers approaching, appeared.

One was calling, 'Fine ribbands of all colours!' and the other was an old, old man croaking, 'Whitstable oysters, all fresh and new!'

There were six riders in all, and Tomas was off his horse the first, standing up in his stirrups and leaping to the ground. He ran to the lady-in-waiting and helped her down from her pony, then (while I wondered if she'd lingered in his arms a little longer than was strictly necessary) led the two horses towards a stable and began speaking to a groom.

I took the opportunity to approach the group.

'A new play at the Curtain!' I said, offering them a bill.

None of them gave any indication of having heard me.

'*The Country Husband*, at the Curtain!'

My rival, who was dressed in a black fur jerkin with embroidered fastenings, turned and glanced at me, and I did not imagine the look of complete disdain on her face. Of course, I was dressed very humble, not in satins and velvets as were her party, nor with hair as deep and shiny a brown as the conkers that boys game with – but there was no reason for her to look at me with such contempt.

She beckoned to the ribband seller and, with the other three ladies of the party, exclaimed over his wares. 'Such colours!' she said, picking up the ribbands and letting them slide through her fingers. Tomas returned and she tossed back her hair and smiled at him. 'Tomas! Do you think a green ribband would suit the colour of my hair?'

'It would suit it very well indeed, Madam – as may be discerned from the many other green ribbands you have already!'

She gave a little pout at this, which pleased me immensely, for to me it meant that Tomas was not in the habit of buying her ribbands. This practice (though I own it may be different in London), if followed at home in Hazelgrove, meant you were practically betrothed, and was at least a sign that you were walking out together.

The ladies turned away from the peddler and began to walk towards the archway I'd come through, while the other male member of the party stopped to speak to a groom. How delightful it would be, I thought, to play a jape on Tomas in return for the many he'd played on me. Seizing my chance and my courage, I called out to him, 'New play at the Curtain!'

He held out his hand and I gave him a playbill. 'And are you a player?' he asked.

'I am, Sire!'

'What part do you act in this play?'

I prayed I was not blushing. 'Just a small part. A maidservant.'

'You play the girls' roles?'

'I do, being . . . er . . . smaller of stature and softer of voice.'

He nodded. 'Indeed. I think that must be the

only place where such qualities are called for in a man.'

'You speak truly,' I said, my heart in my mouth. 'But 'tis a good new play. Perhaps you might come next week with your friends.'

'Perhaps,' he said. 'Will you be taking a part every day?'

'I believe so, Sir.' I gave a short, formal bow, Tomas returned the same and we then turned to go in opposite directions. My heart was thumping furiously. I'd seen him; actually spoken to him – and he hadn't recognised me. Oh, how I'd be able to tease him later!

I reached the archway and a voice called, 'Hey, Lucy!'

Before I could stop myself I turned with the word 'Yes?' on my lips – and there stood Tomas, hands on hips, grinning at me.

'Oh!' I stamped my foot with vexation.

He began laughing. 'Did you think I wouldn't know you?' he asked. 'Did you think that the queen's fool could be fooled quite so easily?'

'But when did you know it was me?'

'Just as soon as we rode up. Before that, even.'

'Truly?'

He nodded. We looked at each other and my heart thumped again.

'Well, Lucy,' he asked very seriously, 'how do you fare here in London?'

'I do very well, I thank you, although the Dee family is not yet arrived.'

'And now I find that you are working for the play-house!'

'I have only just been taken on there because of sickness,' I said, adding hastily, 'and they don't know that I'm a girl!'

''Tis a good disguise,' he said, looking at me closely, 'and one that we can employ, mayhap.' I fought the sudden urge to pull off the coif and let down my hair, knowing I must look awfully plain with not a curl to be seen and not a bit of lace or frill about my person.

'But what of the Scottish queen?' I asked. 'And when will you send for me to do some work for Her Grace again? How does our royal lady? Is her heartache eased somewhat?'

He smiled at my pell-mell of questions. 'The Scottish queen is to be moved to Fotheringay Castle, where she will be watched day and night.'

'So Her Grace is perfectly safe now?'

He shook his head. 'One can never say that, for Walsingham's spies discover new plots at every turn. While Mary of Scotland lives, Her Grace can never be truly safe.'

'Then why doesn't she order her death?' I asked in a low voice.

Tomas shrugged. ''Twould be an awesome and shocking thing for the queen to do, for they are both crowned heads of state and God's anointed. Besides, they are close related: first cousins.'

'But is it still likely that Mary could . . .'

He was shaking his head before I finished. 'You need not be too fearful,' he said, 'for Mary's Catholic followers don't have enough money to raise the army they need in order to overthrow her guard, march on London and take the throne.'

I smiled, relieved about this, at least. 'And what of the other matter? Is Her Grace more composed now? Has she forgiven Robert Dudley?'

'She has not!' He smiled wryly. 'She has banned him and his new wife from Court.'

'Indeed!'

'Although she is somewhat occupied by something else at this moment . . .'

'A new suitor?' I asked eagerly.

He shook his head. 'No, she is well occupied with Sir Francis Drake's treasure, for he's arrived back from a skirmish with such a burden of gold and jewels that his ship rides low in the water.'

I gasped.

'Amongst the treasure there is said to be a diamond which is as big and blue as a plum,' he whispered.

I marvelled at this very much. 'Has he given it to the queen?'

'It's believed that he's given her a share of the cargo: gold and treasure of innumerable worth, but no one is sure if she also has the blue diamond. The value of such a rare and beautiful object would be almost incalculable.'

I shifted the remaining playbills in my hand, wanting to bring the conversation to a more personal level. 'And are you busy in London just now, Tomas?' I asked. 'Does the queen hold as many fête days and masques as she did in Richmond?'

'Not as many – but as spring arrives, there will be more.' In the background, I saw my friend from the royal laundry, Barbara, passing, looking at us curiously. 'And as you know,' Tomas went on, 'the queen much enjoys a new play, so perhaps your company of actors will be requested to perform at Whitehall.'

'I'd very much enjoy that.' I paused and forced my face into a pleasant, enquiring smile. 'And the new lady-in-waiting that you were squiring; has she settled into her position?'

'Mistress Juliette?'

I did not know this was her name, but it was the sort of name I would have expected her to have, so nodded.

'She has settled. Mistress Juliette quite enjoys riding now, and she makes music, composes poetry, embroiders and sings with the other ladies at Court as easily as if she was born to it. Which she was, of course.'

'Of course.' It was an effort to keep the smile on my face, but I believe I managed it. I was about to bid Tomas a reluctant farewell when I heard the thundering of hooves and in a moment a black horse, sweating very much, came around the corner. Its rider – who was dressed in a deep-purple velvet cloak and hat trimmed with silver – slipped off and tossed the reins to Tomas, saying, 'If you please, Sirrah!'

Tomas bowed, half-mockingly, for it was obvious that the rider had mistaken him for a groom.

'See to it that my horse is stabled,' the man continued, then strode off at a fast pace towards the palace.

I looked after him. 'Who was that?'

Tomas grinned, swinging the reins. 'Did you not know him at close quarters? That was Sir Robert Dudley.'

I clapped my hand to my mouth. 'You said he was banned from Court.'

'Banned – yes. But that doesn't prevent him from trying to see Her Grace. And married or no, it is obvious that he still loves her and has her best interests at heart.'

I twisted the groat at my neck. 'Remember that I, too, love the queen and want to serve her,' I said, for being within the grounds of the royal palace and observing the workings of the Court all around me had reminded me of how thrilling it was to be close to Her Grace.

'Your turn will come,' he said. 'And now I must see that this horse is stabled, then go and check what entertainments the queen has asked for tonight.'

We smiled at each other and I, remembering in time that I was still dressed as a lad, did not offer him my hand to kiss.

'I will see you very soon.' He gave a formal bow, winking at me the while, and I returned the same and we parted.

What entertainments would he preside over that night? I wondered all the way home. Little masques and playlets that he would act with Juliette? Pastoral scenes with her dressed as a milkmaid and he a shepherd boy? The new dance from Italy which required the gentleman to clasp the lady around the waist and lift her into the air? In my head, I imagined all these and more, and therefore was not in a good humour when I arrived back at the house in Green Lane.

I went indoors and, stopping to take off my pattens, heard voices in the kitchen and realised that Sonny had returned. Pleased at this, for I had begun worrying about how long he'd been gone, I went down the passageway eager for news. To my surprise I found him sitting hunched up before the fire looking miserable, the track-marks of tears on his face. There was an unpleasant smell in the air; something earthy which I could not quite discern.

'Whatever's the matter, Sonny?' I asked anxiously.

He stuck his bottom lip out and shook his head as if he couldn't speak of the matter.

'He's been pushed about. Had a rough time of it,' Mistress Midge said indignantly. 'When he got to our house in Mortlake, that so-called gent'man Mr Kelly seized hold of him and shook him.'

'Never!'

'Not only shook him, but shouted at him and said that they had no intention of using a street urchin to send their valuable messages!' fumed Mistress Midge. 'The man's a venomous varmint! He swore at you and me for thinking up such a scheme and accused the lad of being a common vagabond.'

'And what of Dr Dee?' I asked. 'What did he have to say?'

Mistress Midge indicated that Sonny should answer, and he gave an enormous sniff and wiped his nose on his jacket sleeve before he did so. 'I didn't see him, but he sent a message to say that I wasn't to come there again. He was all the time in the bedchambers. There was summat happening . . . summat goin' on but I never found out what.'

The cook and I looked at each other.

'That'll be the mistress for sure!' she said.

'Taken ill again?' I asked, for Mistress Dee had never been a particularly robust lady.

'Or worse,' she said darkly.

'What of Merryl and Beth?' I asked Sonny. 'Are they all right?'

Sonny nodded. 'Well enough. They was busy a-doing things with their tutor and didn't speak to me much.'

'I'm sure they would have done if they'd had time . . .'

'No one spoke to me; they just shouted at me. Only

the monkey was pleased to see me. An' . . . an' I had to wait an age to get a boat back here, and when I did it was on a barge that held night soil what they fix up to tip on gardens and it stank summat rotten.'

I sniffed, realising then what the earthy smell was, and Mistress Midge and I exchanged looks of horror.

'Well now,' said Mistress Midge, patting Sonny on the head but keeping a little distance between them, 'how would you like some lovely, tasty gingerbread mice to eat, all warm from the oven and frosted with sugar?'

Sonny brightened up somewhat. 'I'd like that very much, Missus.' He looked around forlornly. 'But how shall I fare now? Where shall I go? Don't send me back to the horspiddle!'

I patted his shoulder tentatively. 'You don't have to go anywhere at the moment. But as soon as we can, we'll find a new place for you.'

'Can't I stay here with you?'

'Maybe not, seeing as Mr Kelly has taken against you,' I said. 'But we'll try and find something close by, so that you can come and see me and Mistress Midge whenever you like.'

'Will you find me somewhere nice?'

'Of course!' Mistress Midge handed Sonny two gingerbread mice and he managed a smile. 'And when you've eaten, then we'll start boiling water and you can have a bath.'

'I've never had one of those,' he said, looking

somewhat anxious.

'You'll like it,' I promised.

As Sonny ate his gingerbread mice, Mistress Midge spoke in a low voice, 'For sure the mistress has miscarried the baby. She was not well enough to bear another so soon after little Arthur.'

'Is that what you think?'

She nodded. 'That's the pattern of her life – I have been with her since she was a babe herself, remember? She gives birth safely, then a miscarriage follows. The next time, all will be well.'

'Poor lady,' I said, wondering how long it would be before she was well enough to travel. 'Twas unkind of me not to wish her a swift return to health, but I knew it would suit me so much better if her recovery was delayed another two weeks or so, for then I'd be able to continue attending the playhouse – and possibly go again to Whitehall Palace.

'How long would a woman take to recover from such a misfortune?' I asked Mistress Midge.

She shrugged. 'It all depends on how well she was to start with. And the mistress has never been strong, we know that.'

'So perhaps two weeks . . .'

'Maybe as long as three,' she said, 'although of course there's nothing to stop Dr Dee and Mr Kelly coming to London on their own.'

'Of course not,' I said, and began praying fervently that they would not.

'In the meantime,' said Mistress Midge, 'what are we to do about the list sent to Dr Dee of all the stuffs we want? What are we supposed to do about getting tradesmen in to fit the house ready for the family?'

I shrugged, shaking my head to say I had no idea. In truth, I was already more worried about being on stage at the Curtain and wondering what I had let myself in for . . .

Chapter Nine

As if in answer to Mistress Midge's worries, however, someone pounded on our front door the next afternoon. When I went to open it there stood a messenger – a lanky chap in a tweed doublet – holding a letter.

'I bring an important missive,' he said, and handed over a folded parchment bearing Dr Dee's seal. 'I was instructed by Dr Dee to tell you to go to the scrivener at the sign of the gold quill, who will read it for you.'

'But I . . .' I began, and then merely curtseyed, hiding a smile as I did so. In spite of writing to Dr Dee in my own hand – and my unformed and scratchy writing could in no way be compared to the scribing of a scrivener – it was obviously beyond Dr Dee's comprehension that a humble maid could read or write. 'I shall do so, Sir, I thank you,' I said.

I did not go anywhere, of course, but took the letter

straight to Mistress Midge, who, as the senior member of our little household, removed the seal, unfolded it and handed it to me.

The letter, in Dr Dee's flowing hand, told us to apply to certain offices in the Strand, where he had appointed an agent, Mr Compton, who would verify any purchases of furniture and also appoint and pay the workmen needed to finish the house. There was no mention of when the family might arrive nor of the condition of Mistress Dee, but of course he wouldn't think to appraise mere servants of these matters.

The following morning Mistress Midge put on her best feathered hat and prepared to take herself off to speak with Mr Compton, and I decided to take Sonny along to the Curtain with me. I thought he would add to my credence as a boy – we could be lads together; brothers.

At first he was horrified at this, and when I told him that I'd been asked to act upon the stage, grew somewhat confused.

'Let's get this right, Missus,' he said. 'You're going to be a girl acting a lad acting a girl.'

'That's right.'

'But 'tis against nature. 'Sides, you don't look like a boy.'

'I don't look like one to you,' I said, 'because you know I'm a girl.' As I spoke I was buttoning up my boyish jacket and pulling on long socks. 'But to anyone seeing me for the first time . . . well, if you see someone dressed as a lad, you naturally think he's a lad.' I turned and tried to catch my reflection in the kitchen window. Not wanting to have my hair scraped back in such an ugly fashion under a coif all the time, the previous night I'd asked Mistress Midge to cut it with her kitchen scissors. It now came down to my ears, which was short for a girl but rather long for a boy.

'What do you think to my hair? Do I look like one of the palace pageboys?' I asked Sonny, but he just sniggered by way of reply.

Dressed and capped to my satisfaction, the thought of the small adventure I was about to embark on put me in such high spirits that I couldn't resist acting the lad all the way to the Curtain. Much to Sonny's dismay I knocked off his cap, chased after a dog and even spent some time looking in the window of a barber-surgeon's shop, pondering aloud whether or not I should go in and be shaved.

He, growing more and more embarrassed, at last turned to me indignantly. 'By your leave, Missus . . .'

'I'm not a missus at present,' I whispered.

'Well then, by your leave, *Sire*, from now on I shall walk several steps in front of you, for at the moment I feels like I'm taking part in a play-acting meself.'

The Curtain was a surprising building, for it had been built especially as a theatre (the first proper one in London, I heard someone say), and was shaped inside as an 'O' with wooden seats all around and the stage jutting out into the audience. It could hold many more people than could stand on the balcony of an inn and would, I was sure, be more agreeable to work in from the actors' point of view.

I found Mr James backstage in the tiring room. This was full to heaving with actors, their wealthy patrons and other hangers-on, some masked, some not, and all dressed exceeding well. Seeing so many notable people about caused me to rather lose my boyish bluster and slip back to being a girl again, but Mr James (who was wearing black velvet edged with gold, and had the largest ruff and the fluffiest beard in the place) was preoccupied and didn't seem to notice.

'I've brought my little brother,' I said, my hand on Sonny's shoulder. 'I thought he might be able to help by standing outside and offering playbills to people.'

'Indeed, indeed!' Mr James said expansively. 'Do go to the front of the building, dear boy, and give assistance where you can.'

Sonny shot an alarmed look at me.

'Off you go,' I said. 'I'll see you at the front after the performance.' I gave a short bow to Mr James and tried to recapture my devil-may-care attitude. 'I am at your disposal, Sire, for whatever part you wish me to play.'

Mr James took a step backwards and looked me up and down. 'I've been thinking about your role today, and believe you may be more suited to act a *lady*.'

I smiled, pleased at this.

'I have you in mind to play Mistress Mistletoe, for so few of our actors are refined enough for such a part.

You'll not actually have any words to say, but we need someone who can move across the stage looking beautiful and engage the audience's emotions. Do you think you could do that? Do you think you could play the female, bewitching and flirtatious, yet rather shy?'

'I'll certainly try, Sir,' I answered.

'Excellent! Our wardrobe mistress will supply you with gown and visage, and then you must ask for a copy of the play from the stage manager and ask him to mark your entrances and exits.'

I nodded and he clapped his hands. 'Run along, then, dear boy.'

The wardrobe mistress, Mistress Hunt, was the only other female in the place and worked from a large curtained-off area in the tiring room surrounded by rails of clothing and baskets of materials.

She looked me up and down and nodded her approval. 'You'll do very well as Mistress Mistletoe. The boy who played her last time was too stout to fit properly into a gown. The one before *that* was so tall that I had to add a flounce to the bottom of his kirtle or you would have seen his hairy ankles.'

I smiled at this and she added, 'You're much better proportioned, young sir, and will make a mighty fine lady.'

Before I could stop myself, I curtseyed to acknowledge this compliment and Mistress Hunt went off into peals of admiring laughter, saying she saw that I was in character already.

It was fortunate that she handed me my petticoats and boned farthingale first, so that I could step into these and remove my breeches under cover, so to speak. I knew it might be slightly more difficult to hide the shape of my upper body, but that morning I'd had the wit to put on a tight, laced bodice which flattened me considerably. I told Mistress Hunt that I intended to leave this in place, saying I had a weak chest and suffered badly with coughs and colds.

Mistress Mistletoe, the wardrobe mistress informed me, was a rich and unhappy young heiress who'd been married for her money and crossed in love. I was to wear a fine gown and accessories, all of which had been donated by a wealthy lady whose husband was a patron of the theatre.

'It's a fine and beautiful outfit and not a year out of fashion!' said Mistress Hunt.

'But why . . .' I began in high-pitched surprise, then lowered my voice to sound more manly. 'But why would she give such a gown to the theatre?'

'Bless you for being a lad!' said the wardrobe mistress. 'Don't you know the aristocracy will not wear anything that's even slightly out of date? As soon as news of the latest fashion arrives from Paris, they have to have their wardrobes updated.'

'But why don't they *sell* their clothes?' I asked in amazement, for I knew that the market in garments was such that they might be sold on for years and years, their fabrics becoming weaker and more delicate until even the poorest beggar couldn't wear them and they were sold for cleaning rags.

'The greatest of our ladies have no need of money,' Mistress Hunt scoffed.

'Then surely the kind thing to do would be to pass their unwanted gowns on to their ladies-in-waiting?'

She shook her head. 'Servants – even a great lady's servants – are not allowed to wear luxurious fabrics or deep colours. Did you not know that only a countess may wear cloth of gold or purple silk, and only a baron's wife can wear silver lace, and a knight's wife embroidered taffeta? Oh, there is no end to the rules and regulations about these things.'

I shook my head in surprise. 'But whose orders are these?'

'The queen's. So the great ladies who patronise the theatre pass on the gowns they deem unfashionable to their favourite group of players. And that is our great fortune!'

When she unwrapped the bodice, kirtle and sleeves I was to wear I was quite overwhelmed and speechless, for they were the most beautiful garments I'd ever seen (apart, perhaps, from those heavily jewelled and embroidered gowns worn by Her Grace). The material was billowing silver tissue and the centre of the kirtle was ruched back to show a frontispiece of heavily embroidered lace which matched that on the bodice and hem.

'What do you think?' said Mistress Hunt.

I gasped out a few words, and then tried to curb my fervour a little, knowing that a lad would not be so overcome by a mere gown.

'And there are jewels and pearls that will further enhance you.'

'And are those . . . ?'

She laughed. 'No, alas. The great ladies do not patronise us to that extent, to give us their gemstones.' She looked at my hair and shook her head slightly. 'But your hair will not do, so we must find you a wig and some hair ornaments and a pretty fan.' She smiled at me. 'It's mighty pleasurable to be able to dress a boy who has so many girlish attributes. Let's hope that you don't grow too stocky and man-like as you get older.'

'Yes, let's hope that,' I said, with more meaning behind my words than she could ever know.

By the time Mistress Hunt had finished, my dear old ma would not have known me. Indeed, when I looked in the polished steel mirror that hung on the wall of the tiring room, I hardly knew myself, for apart from the beauty of the gown, my wig, fair as summer corn, was now finished with ribbands and combs, my feet were daintily shod in silver slippers and my neck was adorned with ropes of pearls. I looked every inch the rich young heiress I was supposed to be.

I only had to come on to the stage twice, and both times but briefly, so it hardly seemed worth the tremendous effort it took to prepare me. However, it seemed my new persona was popular amongst the audience, for as soon as I stepped nervously on stage (where I had to pretend to discover my betrothed deep in conversation with another lady), they began clapping and stamping on the ground, and someone even threw flowers. I was not vain enough to take this admiration personally, however, for I knew that they were merely applauding the seemingly remarkable transformation of the boy that they thought I was, into a girl. How I'd have loved my ma to have seen me dressed thus, though, and my sisters, and most of all, perhaps, Isabelle, whom I knew would relish hearing every last detail of my gown.

After the performance I was asked to go into the tiring room to mingle with the vast multitude of admirers who'd come to pay their respects to the players, and at this time I was immediately approached by two other actors who'd played women. They seized me and were determined to make a great fuss of me, linking arms and pledging that they were going to be my close and special best friends.

I found this amusing at first – and indeed they were very funny and droll with their rouged cheeks and drawn-on eyelashes – but they seemed to see themselves as rivals for my attention and began to squabble about which one I liked the best, so I became rather embarrassed. When someone tapped me on the shoulder, therefore, I was more than ready to leave the dispute that had broken out and was only a little surprised (for my meetings with him always seemed to be unexpected) when, on turning around, I saw Tomas and Juliette standing before me.

They were both masked, but I knew Tomas masked or not now, and recognised Juliette because of her beautiful hair, gleaming with chestnut lights under the candles and easily outshining all the wigs and false-hair switches in the room.

Facing them, I immediately sank into a curtsey, but to my great astonishment *she* sank into an even deeper one. I rose, but she remained in position for a moment longer than I did, which caused me so much wonder that I believe my jaw dropped open in surprise, for the strange and wonderful dream I'd had was come true.

As she rose, I couldn't help but notice that Tomas was hiding a smile as he introduced us. 'Mistress Juliette Mackenzie, Mistress Lucy Walden,' he said.

Juliette inclined her head to me gracefully. 'May I compliment you on your gown, Madam. It's by far the most beautiful in the room.'

'Thank you,' I said, rather surprised, 'but . . .'

'And Mistress Juliette especially admired your jewels,' interrupted Tomas, still with the half-smile on his lips. 'We saw them glittering across the tiring room and she insisted on being brought to see them at close quarters.'

'Yes . . .' I began again.

'The emerald in your hair decoration is a most excellent size,' Juliette said breathlessly, ''tis almost as large as the Taja emerald owned by the queen.'

'But the queen's emeralds are real!' I had to say. 'This is not. Neither are the diamonds at my wrists nor the pearl necklaces.'

She looked at me, astounded. '*None* of your jewellery is real?'

I touched the coin around my neck, which had been completely concealed by the mass of pearls Mistress Hunt had fitted me out with. 'Apart from this groat.'

She looked at it in astonishment and not a little disgust.

'I am decked out in all these to play the part of Mistress Mistletoe,' I explained. 'Didn't you see me on the stage?'

Tomas shook his head. 'Unfortunately we were delayed at Whitehall. We took a carriage and set off as quickly as we could – for I was anxious to see your stage debut – but I fear we missed you. We only caught the last half-hour of the performance.'

'I see,' I said. I hadn't noticed anyone arriving late but this was not remarkable because – as had happened before – the audience had moved around throughout the play; changing seats, standing up and coming and going with much laughter and banter between them and the players. 'I was on stage twice,' I said, rather regretting that Tomas hadn't seen me.

'Then unfortunately we missed you twice.'

Juliette had been staring in astonishment from one to the other of us during this conversation. 'So you are an *actor*?' she asked at last. 'And all the jewels and accessories you wear are false?'

'I'm afraid they are,' I admitted.

She looked disappointed, then rallied. 'Then by your leave, Sir, you make a mighty fine lady. Almost as fine as my patron and aunt, Lady Margaret Ashe.'

'Your aunt is Lady Ashe?' I asked in surprise and some excitement. 'Then you are indeed fortunate, for she's a fine and noble lady.' I didn't add that she lived close to my home village and that once I almost worked for her as a maid.

Tomas began to laugh and I could not help but do likewise, for usually I was the one who was being teased and it felt a good deal better to be in on the joke. He coughed behind his hand. 'Mistress Juliette, there's something else about the mighty fine Mistress Mistletoe that you should know . . .'

I looked about us, but the two 'women' who'd been pursuing me had left to go and annoy someone else and there was so much talk and bluster in the room that no one would overhear us. I was sorry, however, that she had to know, for I very much liked the idea of Tomas and I sharing a secret.

'And what is that?' Juliette asked.

'She is not a he.'

Juliette stared, first at him, then at me. 'What do you mean?'

'Or should I say he is not a she?'

Juliette tutted with annoyance.

'I beg your leave to explain,' I said in a low voice.

'What Tomas means is that although this company of players think I am a boy, I am actually a girl.'

'A female actor?' she gasped. 'Never!' She fluttered the fan she carried. 'I am truly appalled!'

'But 'tis not so shocking, surely,' I said, 'for on feast days the ladies of the Court – and even Her Grace – take part in masques and plays.'

'But what the aristocracy do is a thing apart. And besides, *you* are not a lady of the Court!'

'By your leave, I am not,' I admitted.

She fluttered the fan some more. 'But how did this come about?'

'I went to a play disguised as a boy,' I explained, 'and Mr James picked me out in the crowd as someone he thought could act a girl's part.'

'But had you knowledge of the stage? What are you in real life?'

'I'm a nursemaid,' I said simply.

She looked over her fan at me, rather as if she had a bad smell under her nose.

'Lucy is nursemaid to Dr Dee's children,' Tomas explained. 'We met in Mortlake – you may remember I stopped to speak to her on the roadway as we rode out.'

'I really don't recall.'

'She has assisted me once or twice in different ways, and will no doubt do so again. She can be trusted in all things, for she has a particular love of Her Grace.'

'As do we all . . .' murmured Juliette. She stared at me coldly, unblinkingly, no doubt wondering how I looked when I was myself, without the jewels and the hairpiece and the glorious gown (and probably coming to the only truth: that I could not hold a candle to her).

'But we must go,' Tomas said to me, 'and not keep you from your friends and players.'

I looked round to see the two 'women' bearing down on us, waving what looked like a bottle of Rhenish. One had his wig of golden curls tipped slightly to one side, showing a bald patch beneath.

'But won't you stay?' I asked.

Tomas shook his head. 'Sadly, we cannot. The queen is entertaining a deputation of gentlemen from Ireland.'

'So we have a party of our own to attend,' Juliette said. 'I must go and put on my finest gown. And my *real* jewels!' she added with a sweet smile.

'We will see you again soon, Lucy,' Tomas said. 'Her Grace is minded to have a picnic in St James's Park to celebrate spring, and would have the Queen's Players perform for her. I've already spoken to Mr James, so if you're still with the players when this takes place . . .'

'I certainly hope to be,' I said.

We said our goodbyes and I dropped a deep curtsey to them both. Tomas bowed in return, but of course Juliette did not return this compliment now that she knew my humble status, but merely nodded at me and turned on her heels. I'd had my moment, though, just as my dream had foretold, and had very much enjoyed it.

Chapter Ten

I could not play the actor for the next few days, so I felt very dull. The agent that Dr Dee had appointed visited the house and gave instructions to various workmen to replaster, paint and repair as he saw fit. I was kept busy moving those of the master's books we'd brought with us from place to place so that they didn't get marked or dusty, and also watching the workmen so that they didn't slacken in their duties or steal away with anything. I sent Sonny to Mr James with apologies for my absence, fearing I might lose my place with them, but he returned with a verbal message (which he delivered in Mr James's grand style) to say that Richard James, actor-manager, sent his compliments and would be happy to see me whenever it suited.

Sonny was gone for some time on this errand and eventually arrived back to explain that he was late because Mistress Hunt had asked him to help sort out her dressing-pins.

'I had to upend her work-basket on the floor and sort the pins into boxes of small, middling and large,' he said proudly. 'It took a long time but she said I did it very nice and proper. When I'd finished, she gave me a big slice of pumpkin pie for me trouble. She's nice, she is.'

I smiled, pleased he was happy and making himself useful, but a little concerned as to what would become of him once Dr Dee and Mr Kelly arrived in London.

Having time on my hands meant I had more leisure to think about things, and my thoughts were divided pretty evenly between Tomas on the one hand and Ma on the other. When I was not fretting about one (did Tomas care about me? How, then, did he feel about Mistress Juliette?), I was filled with anxiety about the other (was Ma managing to stay out of the workhouse? How was my father treating her?). These worries lodged themselves in my head and it did not seem that they would be easily resolved.

The following week I had a note from Tomas – a rather formal and correct note. It asked, provided Mistress Midge could spare me, if I would spend Friday dressed as a boy, working as a stable hand at Whitehall Palace.

There is a tilt planned for Saturday and the stables are being cleaned in readiness, the note said. *One ostler more or less will not be noticed amid the servants, and you may overhear something which will be of use to us in our continual endeavours against Her Grace's enemies.*

I searched the note carefully for something personal or the mark 'X', which I knew meant a kiss, but looked in vain. Still, I thought, I was sure to see him there, and at least he must be thinking about me to send for me.

Mistress Midge, fortunately, had always shown a surprising lack of curiosity about what I did outside the house, and, as I'd been very helpful to her by more than once going out selling her sugared mice on a tray, was happy to let me have time off.

Unlike, probably, any other stable hand that day, I spent a considerable amount of time planning how I should look, wanting to look authentic yet not too unattractive. When it came down to it, however, I still only had Mistress Midge's old jacket and Sonny's breeches to wear, but I topped these with a battered flat cap found in the street (a remnant of a struggle between two groups of rival apprentices) and put a red paisley kerchief around my neck inside my white shirt. Thus clothed, I set off very early on Friday and was at the palace stables before seven of the clock in the morning, ready, in the service of our queen, to garner as much information as I could.

I found the stable yards full of men, youths and horses; more horses than I'd ever seen together before, large and glossy and in colours from black to white and every shade of brown in between. As I mingled there it struck me that, although supposedly a stable hand, I did not know how to care for a horse: at which end to start grooming and which broom, brush or polisher to use where (for at least I knew there were certain conventions about such things). However, I soon realised that these aristocrats' horses were mightily prized, highly expensive animals and each one had a dedicated set of ostlers who'd no more allow a common servant boy to touch their precious horse than they'd allow a beggar to sup at their table. I did not have to worry, either, about not looking as if I belonged, for many extra staff had been taken on to cope with the numbers coming for the joust the following day and everyone seemed to presume I belonged to someone else.

I made myself busy carrying buckets from pump to stables and back again, and as I carried I listened. I heard talk about the queen and Sir Robert Dudley (though nothing that I didn't know already), about Mary, Queen of Scotland, and the place where she was currently imprisoned – and also heard some interesting new gossip about the varied and colourful love life she'd enjoyed. I heard much about Sir Francis Drake – on the one part regarding whether or not he'd presented the queen with the blue diamond, and on the other some speculation as to whether he was a serious contender for her hand. A swarthy blacksmith's lad insisted to me that, Drake being somewhat of a hero figure because of all he'd plundered, was well worthy of the queen, while his master was equally insistent that because Drake was younger than Her Grace and from a humble background, he must be ruled out. Listening to all these opinions and speculation, I reached the conclusion that men enjoyed to gossip every bit as much as women did.

When I joined in with this tittle-tattle, sometimes I came down on one side of the fence and sometimes on the other. I dearly wanted the queen to be happily married, but didn't always commend her choice. Drake, for instance, was said to be very haughty (I heard several people say it that day), and to my mind this is one of the worst traits anyone can have, for just saying the word puts me in mind of Mr Kelly. And so I went on listening at stable doors and hanging around whenever I saw men deep in conversation, but at no time did I hear anything disparaging said about Her Grace, hear the Catholic faith commended, nor overhear anyone saying that we should be ruled by Mary instead of Elizabeth.

I would, I feared, have little news to tell Tomas when I saw him.

As the day went on and people got used to my face I was given the occasional job to do: mucking out a stable, heaving weighty tack from one place to another or lugging bales of hay around, and I tried to do these while whistling and acting as carefree as a real lad, even though I often felt like collapsing under the weight of a particularly heavy saddle or straw bundle.

In the afternoon I found some time to cross the grounds of the palace and go and see the tilting yard, which I thought was a great marvel, being long and as wide as the road to London, and lined on each side with gaily painted stands containing rows of seats. In the centre of these stands was a kind of tented gallery bright with decorated wooden shields and having carved chairs within holding embroidered silk cushions. This place, I knew from engravings, was where the queen and her ladies would sit to watch the jousting, and it was here that the magnificently armoured knights would come to ask for a favour: a glove or a kerchief from their chosen lady to tie on to their lance.

''Tis a wonderful sight when the galleries are full, the pennants are fluttering and the knights are pacing about on their horses,' a voice beside me said, and I looked round to see my laundress friend, Barbara, smiling at me.

Her eyes widened in surprise when she realised who I was. 'Why, 'tis you, Master Luke the actor!' she said.

I nodded and gave a short bow of greeting, pulling my cap down a little further as I did so.

She returned a curtsey. 'But what are you doing here today – and carrying a bucket instead of a bill?'

I hesitated a moment. Spies, we all knew, were everywhere: spies from foreign countries looking for excuses to wage war on England, spies for Mary of Scotland, and spies to find out who was faithful within the queen's household. I did not, however, want her to know that I was there to listen to others' conversations, so I smiled and crossed my fingers ready to tell a lie. 'You may think it strange,' I said, 'but I have to play an ostler on stage soon and I don't know anything about horses. I came here so that I might become more at ease with them.'

'You have never ridden a horse?'

I shook my head. 'Not properly. Never held the reins.'

'So you're here to learn which end to feed and which end to avoid!'

We both laughed. 'Then is there to be a real horse with you on stage?'

I nodded, then went on quickly, 'But what of you? Did you find anyone to take you to the play?'

'I did not,' she said. She looked at me wistfully. 'I seldom meet a nice lad, for they are either too busy serving the queen, or are followers of one of her ladies-in-waiting and fail to see any attraction in anyone else.'

'The queen's ladies certainly are all very fine,' I said, which I own was not tactful of me.

'Ah, but most are empty-headed flibbertigibbets without the sense of a weasel,' she said with a sniff. 'Oh, they look very fine – but 'tis strange to me that a youth cannot see beyond ribbands and ruffles!'

This answer was so close to my own way of thinking that I was tempted to laugh and squeeze her arm in empathy. Instead I said, 'Some youths can see beyond those.'

At this she beamed at me and I realised, too late, that she had taken my words as a sign of interest in her. 'Then, Master Luke,' she said, 'will you come into the kitchens and take some refreshment?'

'I am not sure . . .' I said cautiously. For though I was feeling hungry enough to eat a dish of boiled turnips, I was worried: firstly that I might not pass too close an inspection as a boy, and secondly that she, in flirting with me, was soon going to put me in a difficult position.

'Oh, do come!' She winked. 'Cook has an eye for a nice young lad.'

This decided me. 'I fear I can't spare the time,' I said. 'I must carry on here a little longer seeing how everyone works, and then return to the theatre.'

Her face fell. 'Then is there nothing I can do for you?'

I shook my head. 'I think not, I thank you.'

'Perhaps one day you might have to act a laundry maid, and then I can give you instruction on how to iron the queen's ruffs.'

I laughed. '*Do* you iron the queen's ruffs?'

'I have done, but only the once,' she said. 'Her two personal laundry maids were ill and I am known to be nimble-fingered, so the Lady of the Queen's Bedchamber sent for me. I had to wash and pleat a special organdie ruff that Her Grace wanted to wear that day.'

'And did you see her?'

'Sadly, I did not, for she was in her inner chamber preparing herself and having her hair dressed.' She lowered her voice to a whisper, 'They do say that Her Grace wears a wig now.'

I nodded, for I had heard this too. 'Were you there long? Did you see anyone else of note?'

'I was there for over two hours, pleating and starching and using a goffering iron to make the ruff just right, and during that time saw a good many of her ladies going about their duties.'

'Did you like them?'

She wriggled her nose. 'I liked those who were nice to me and misliked those who were not. Some spoke kindly, and some were aloof.'

I hesitated for a moment, then asked, 'Did you see a Mistress Juliette?'

Barbara nodded. 'She of the brown eyes and long auburn hair.' She looked at me sideways. 'Is it she who draws your admiration, Sir?'

'God's teeth, no!' I said, swearing manfully. 'I merely had the honour of seeing her when she came to the Curtain with the queen's fool to arrange an entertainment.'

'She is very fair of face . . .'

'Oh, perhaps, perhaps,' I said carelessly. 'Her patron is Lady Ashe, who lived very near to me at home. Was Mistress Juliette one of those who spoke to you kindly?'

She shook her head. 'She was not – and I own I didn't care for her.'

I looked at her enquiringly and she was only too ready to tell me what had occurred. 'I was sitting in a little closet on my own quietly folding the last of the pleats – which are always the most difficult and fiddling – when she came by. She likes to know what's going on, that one! She asked me how long I'd been on my own there and if I'd overheard anything of interest.'

'Really?'

'Indeed! She was most insistent that I tell her who'd been in the outer rooms and wanted to know if I'd heard what had gone on earlier – for apparently the queen had that morning entertained Sir Francis Drake.'

'And what did you say?'

'I told the truth – that I'd not heard anything, nor seen anyone apart from some maids of honour. And then she asked if I'd overheard their talk, and if, perhaps, they'd mentioned that jewel they call Drake's Diamond and whether it was in the queen's owner-ship.'

'Really?' I was somewhat puzzled at this.

'I can see you are confused, Master Luke, whereas I was not,' said Barbara, 'for I know that in London all rich young ladies' heads are stuffed with nothing but jewels, hair ornaments and prinking themselves up in the latest Paris fashions. As soon as the queen appears in a new outfit, the rest of the Court has to have it! Why, I believe they think more of jewelled tiaras than they do their own flesh and blood.'

'So she was just . . .'

'She is nothing but air and feathers!' Barbara said roundly. 'An empty-headed flirt-wench!'

'Do you think so?' I said with some pleasure, telling myself that Tomas's head could surely not be turned by a silly creature whose only interests in life were jewels and gee-gaws.

'I do! And you'd be far better off, young master, to stop mooning about such as she and set your sights on a wholesome and honest maidservant. Why, a girl like Mistress Juliette would not share a bowl of milk with a penniless actor like you!'

I laughed. 'I am aware of that – and can assure you that I have absolutely no intention of paying suit to Mistress Juliette.' And for once, I thought as I bade her farewell, I was being absolutely truthful.

I left by the main square and found that a small group of people was watching the antics of a Harlequin with a painted face and diamond-patterned suit, who was turning somersaults at an alarming speed around the fountain, flipping over and over with great neatness and agility. He completed a full circuit, landed on his feet and bowed deeply. The small audience applauded and – as he took off his short cloak and threw it down for them to throw money on to – moved off quickly.

I smiled as I approached him, for I was sure it was Tomas, even though his face was quartered blue-and-white and he wore a mask. I needed to hear him speak to be completely sure, for once someone had come up to me dressed identically and I'd almost been tricked.

'Lucy! It *is* me,' he said in Tomas's own, true voice.

'So it is,' I said. 'But why are you out here doing cartwheels around the fountain?'

'I thought to see you before you went home.' He looked at me searchingly and I felt myself blush with pleasure, so that he made a show of standing back and frowning at me. 'Male cheeks do not usually turn pink!' he said with mock severity.

I smiled. 'I'm afraid that I've not yet taken on every aspect of a lad's temperament. But seeing me can't be the only reason you're putting on this performance.'

'You're right,' he said. 'There is a party of acrobats here from the French Court who take every opportunity to make a great show of themselves, and feeling my position was being usurped, I decided that the queen's own fool should give a display.'

I laughed. 'I hope they were impressed.'

He took a quick look about us. 'But what of you? Did you overhear anything of interest in your day as a stable hand?'

I shook my head. 'Nothing that might concern anyone who loves the queen. I heard plenty about Sir Robert Dudley, and about Her Grace's romances and her jewels, but there was nothing amiss – and no word of support for the Scottish queen.'

'That's good.'

'Then is the queen's position safe?'

'The head that bears the crown is never safe,' he said. 'The support for Mary goes on beneath the surface. It's as well that they have not the money to raise an army.'

He was thoughtful for a moment and then asked

me a rather curious question. 'I believe you made gloves before you worked for Dr Dee?'

I nodded. 'I probably made a pair of gloves every day of my life from the time I was seven years old until when I left home.'

'Then tell me, which is more suitable a gift for a lady: a leather or a satin glove?'

'It all depends on what they are to be used for,' I said. 'Leather is more durable, but silk or satin are more romantic, especially if the gloves are scented with almond oil. Do you need them for a special occasion?'

'Well, 'tis St Valentine's Day tomorrow,' he answered. I looked at him blankly and he went on, ''Tis a day for romance; the day when birds are said to choose their mates, did you not know that?'

'I may have heard something . . . but 'tis not a day that we ever celebrated in Hazelgrove.'

'Here at Court it's a custom for the first person of the opposite sex whom you see in the morning to be your sweetheart for the day. The gentleman is then supposed to present the lady with a little gift: a pair of gloves or a flowered kerchief – and there will be a party later, with pairing games and dancing.'

''Tis a pretty thought,' I said, hiding the sting of jealousy I felt.

'And of course every courtier hopes he's not first in the *queen's* sight, or he'll find himself having to buy something rather more extravagant than a pomander ball!'

I laughed at this. 'I shall take care, then, that I am not in boy's costume tomorrow morning,' I said, and we bowed at each other before I left.

Halfway home it struck me. Why shouldn't I be the first person who Tomas saw on the morrow? Why shouldn't I go to Whitehall Palace very early, with a message for him, and thus be his valentine for the day?

Chapter Eleven

I thought about this plan all the way back to Green Lane, and made up my mind that I *would* go, that there was nothing to stop me rising at first call from the watchman, going to the palace and arriving with the milkmaids under the pretence that I had an important message for Tomas. When he saw me it wouldn't matter that I did *not* have a message; for I'd tell him straight that I was there so he could be my valentine. He'd laugh to see me (so my daydream went on) and we'd walk in the orchard together under the budding blossom, then he'd take me to one of the little shops that surrounded the palace and buy me some gloves. I'd choose primrose-yellow satin, I thought, and musing on this possible scene turned into Green Lane and there saw Mistress Midge standing at the door holding something in her hand, with Sonny perched beside her on the window sill. Both were looking anxiously up and down the lane – for me, I presumed – and seeing them I had the feeling that the little adventure I'd planned for the next day was, alas, not going to happen.

Sonny saw me, gave a shout, then jumped down and leapt around me, trying to knock my cap off.

Mistress Midge called for him to behave himself. 'Haven't I got enough worry waiting around for Lucy to return, without you getting yourself into fights with other boys?' I heard her say.

'It *is* me, Mistress Midge!' I said.

I went closer and she first peered at me, then lifted off my cap. 'Bless me, of course it is!'

'What are you holding?' I asked, although I could already see it was a letter with Dr Dee's seal on the back.

'An important document,' she said, 'and I was thinking that if you didn't come back soon, I'd have to go to the scrivener and have it read to me.'

As I took the letter I sent out a fervent prayer that it wasn't going to say that the Dee family were just about to join us in London, for that would be an end to all my fun.

It was not quite this bad. It said:

A volume, Ancient Incantations, *has been taken to London in error and must be returned. It is a book with a green leather cover embossed with a symbol of a black raven. Ensure that it is brought with all haste by Mistress Midge or the girl.*

Mistress Midge gave a snort of derision. 'I knew he'd

get muddled as to which book is where,' she said. 'You mark my words, those books of his will be going up and downriver faster than a fiddler's elbow. *That's* why they should have allowed us to have Sonny as a messenger.'

'*Ancient Incantations*,' I said. 'I wonder what he needs that for . . .'

'That's for him to know and us to wonder.'

'So will you or . . . ?'

'You'll go, of course,' she said, thus putting paid to my plans. 'These bones of mine are too old to enjoy rattling about on a cart to Mortlake – and they won't care for the damp of another river journey, neither.'

So it was decided. She insisted that I set off straight away, so while I, feeling rather low-spirited, changed into my usual old workaday clothes and placed a few things in my cloth bag, she went through Dr Dee's books to find the green volume inscribed with a raven.

This, once discovered, was enormously heavy, with a wooden cover and sturdy brass hinges and fastenings, so Sonny (leaving off eating for a moment) fashioned a means whereby I could carry it by criss-crossing string around it several times and making a handle. We then had to decide by which route I should travel to Mortlake and came to the conclusion that I should go to Puddle Dock and see in which direction the tide was flowing. If it was going upriver, I might find a craft sailing towards Richmond that very evening. If not, I'd either try to hitch a lift on a wagon going that way or wait until the tide turned.

I set off for the river, going on a circular walk which took me past the palace in the hopes that I might see Tomas and explain that I was going away. I did not catch sight of him, however, and so (for I caught the tide) had to endure a seemingly endless journey on a barge drawn by heavy horses, miserably imagining how Juliette would contrive to have Tomas for her valentine and what might happen later during the course of the dancing and pairing games that he'd spoken of.

The barge arrived at Hammersmith Wharf in the coldest, darkest hours of the early morning, and here I found a corner and huddled into my cloak to wait for sunrise before I began walking the four or so miles along the towpath to Mortlake. As I did so I could not help but think about Tomas, for just a short time ago we'd ridden along this very path towards Putney, with me sitting at the front of his horse, his arms tight around me. There had been no sign of Mistress Juliette then; no worries that he might prefer another.

I heard the watchman call eleven of the clock as I passed through Barnes, and, as I came round the river's bend in Mortlake and approached the magician's house, I felt a shiver, for it was as if my senses had played a trick and I was seeing it again for the first time. There it stood as it had long stood: dark, deeply thatched with tangled weeds up to the kitchen window – and in front of it, just as before, Beth and Merryl playing in the silt and mud on the riverbank like commoners' children.

I put Dr Dee's precious book down on the grass and

clapped my hands. 'Beth! Merryl! What are you doing down there?'

They started on hearing me, and, calling excitedly, scrambled up the bank and flung their arms around me. I was touched by this, but also conscious that I only had one kirtle to wear. I bade them stand back, therefore, and promised that there could be more hugs later, when their hands were clean.

I looked them over. They seemed to be wearing a strange assortment of clothes and had nothing on their feet. 'You have no stockings on! And where are your shoes?'

'We took them off so they wouldn't get muddy,' Beth said.

'Surely that was sensible?' Merryl asked.

'But your feet must be frozen. Come inside immediately to wash and put your slippers on.'

They began to wipe their feet on the grass, squealing occasionally with excitement when they glanced at me and saying how happy they were that I'd come.

'For we haven't been doing at all well without you,' Merryl said. She frowned. 'Why is your hair so short?'

''Tis the fashion in London,' I answered.

'You look just like a boy!' she said, and I smiled at this.

'Oh, do come back here and look after us,' Beth pleaded, 'because Mistress Allen is perfectly hateful!'

'She does nothing but complain to our mother about us,' said her sister.

'And Mama does nothing but *cry*,' Beth added despairingly.

'But who cooks for you? And who cleans the house? Who gets you up in the mornings and pins you into your clothes?'

'Mistress Allen dresses us,' Beth began.

'And deliberately sticks pins in us whenever she can!' continued Merryl. 'There are two girls from the village who are supposed to cook and clean, but sometimes they just don't arrive.'

'If they *do*, they sit around giggling with each other.'

'And they steal things! They go home with our sugar in their pockets.'

'But what happens when they don't turn up to work? How do you eat?'

'We nearly starve . . .' said Beth in a melancholy voice.

'No, Father or someone else sends to the tavern for a pigeon pie,' said the less dramatic Merryl.

I picked up the precious book and the girls led the way through the back door into the big kitchen, which was chaotic – but not that much more chaotic than the way it had been when I'd first arrived at the house back in September. As then, what seemed like every bowl, pan, porringer and utensil in the house lay piled and scattered along the table and cupboards, and also, as then, the monkey was hiding inside a kettle and immediately flew at me, chattering like mad, running up over my head and pulling at my hair.

Having short hair was an advantage with a monkey, and I carefully picked off his little hands and handed him to Merryl, bidding her to keep hold of him. I then reached for the kettle and, finding it empty, muttered under my breath about the worthlessness of the kitchen maids (for even the most slatternly girl knows that a kettle over a fire should always be full). Filling it from the bucket, I realised that the fire was about to go out and, finding no wood indoors, donned a long apron and went into the courtyard to search for sticks to build it up again.

Coming back from the courtyard through the hallway with my apron full of wood, the library door opened and Dr Dee appeared. I curtseyed as well as I could, and wished him good-day.

'What are you doing here?' he asked gruffly.

'You sent for someone to bring you a book, Sir,' I said.

'Ah yes,' he replied, though I believe his head was stuffed so full of mystic calculations that he must have forgotten.

'That was two days ago,' came Mr Kelly's voice from within the library. 'Couldn't you have brought it any sooner?'

'I got a space on a barge and came as quickly as I could.' I added a fraction later, 'Sir.'

'Well, girl, where *is* the book?' Dr Dee asked.

'I'll fetch it directly,' I said, and hurried into the kitchen, where I deposited half the wood on the fire, brushed down my apron and skirts and carried the book through to the library.

Within the dimly lit library the air was thick with sulphur, enough to make me cough, and there was another smell which I believe was coming from a jar of silvery liquid bubbling on the alembic over a flame. Mr Kelly was seated at the table with a book open in front of him, his peevish face frowning.

'If we'd had that book earlier we might have succeeded,' he said to Dr Dee.

'Ah. Even then I don't know if all these efforts . . .'

'We can try again, of course, and follow their precise instructions.'

Dr Dee crossed to his desk and sat down, running his fingers absent-mindedly across the top of the skull that always stood there. 'But we have no more tin to hand.'

Tin, I thought, and knew from this that they were again attempting to make gold.

'Just put the book down, girl!' said Dr Dee.

I did so. 'Do you want me to return to London now, Sir, to carry on preparing the new house for your arrival?' I asked, and then hesitated, for much as I longed to go back, I knew my first loyalties should be to my two little charges. 'Or should I stay here for a day or so to help with the domestic arrangements?'

He nodded. 'Yes. Do that,' he said, rather surprising me. 'The mistress is unwell and Beth and Merryl are probably somewhat neglected, though I cannot spare the time to think on what they need.' His face suddenly cleared. 'But I have the very solution to this problem: you may return to London straight away – and take them with you! Yes, that is an excellent notion.'

I nodded and said certainly I would, but as I did so my heart sank, for though I loved both girls dearly, once they were in London and in my charge, that would be an end to all my exploits with the acting company and the freedom to come and go on whatever missions Tomas asked of me.

'Off you go, then, no shilly-shallying,' Mr Kelly said, waving me off.

Feeling rather gloomy, I went back to the kitchen ready to pack up the girls and their possessions and return to London at first tide.

Chapter Twelve

I tapped on the door of Mistress Dee's bedchamber
very gently. There being no reply, I put my ear to it,
tapped again and waited.

I heard nothing, and stood there in somewhat of a
dilemma, for though (after eating a quick meal of stale
bread and cheese; all there was in the pantry) I'd
already given Beth and Merryl the task of selecting the
things they wanted to take with them to London, I
didn't feel I could just leave the house without Mistress
Dee being informed. I had no idea, however, how well
that lady was or what state of mind she was in. I did not
even know whether, as Mistress Midge had surmised,
she *had* miscarried.

On the third knock the door was answered by
Mistress Allen. She was pale, frowning, and wearing
her customary dun-coloured gown with loose jacket.
Over her shoulder I could see into the darkened room,

in the centre of which stood Mistress Dee's silk-hung four-poster bed, its curtains closed.

Mistress Allen looked me up and down in some surprise. 'You're back here?' she said in a whisper. 'Why is this?'

I bobbed a curtsey. 'I was asked to bring a book for Dr Dee. A volume that he'd sent to London by mistake.'

'And now you're returning there?'

I nodded. 'And Dr Dee has asked that I take Beth and Merryl with me.'

I did not imagine the slight lightening of her expression. 'An excellent idea. And the infernal monkey too, I hope.'

I certainly didn't want to take *him*, so didn't commit myself to this. I said, 'I thought it best that I should inform Mistress Dee before we set off.'

Mistress Allen adjusted the net coif which covered her hair. 'She's not well enough to see you, but I shall tell her myself.'

'Is she . . . did she lose a child?'

She nodded briefly. 'But with God's help will recover from her ordeal soon.'

'And then you will follow us to London. Will that be in a week or so, do you think?' I asked, trying to gauge how much more time I had.

Mistress Allen raised her eyebrows, as much as to say what business was it of mine. 'In a week or a month, as long as it takes for Milady to be well enough to travel.'

'I only ask because her well-being will be the first thing that Mistress Midge asks me about,' I said smoothly. 'And of course we need to ensure that all is in readiness for her coming.'

Mistress Allen began to close the door. 'I shall tell Milady straight away. You may bring Merryl and Beth before you go; she'll want to see them to say goodbye.'

She closed the door on my curtsey and I turned to go back along the corridor and down the stairs, passing all the doors and thinking about how, when I'd first arrived at the magician's house straight from our tiny cottage in Hazelgrove, I'd thought that – with its two staircases, endless corridors and many, many rooms – this must surely be the biggest dwelling in the world. It was not, however. Not even nearly, for I'd seen many bigger and wealthier houses since then.

I paused at the turn of the stairs to look out on the churchyard of St Mary's, where once, in the dead of night, I'd seen Dr Dee and Mr Kelly endeavouring to raise the spirit of someone who'd been laid to rest. I smiled as I recalled this, for I'd been somewhat gullible then and imagined that such a thing were possible. Now I knew better than to believe in raising ghosts, for such a thing was – surely? – against Nature's law and God's word.

I carried on going down and had almost reached the kitchen when I heard, from upstairs, a loud scream. And then another and another.

I turned and ran back up again, then hesitated

outside the mistress's door, for even in what seemed like an urgent matter I did not dare to rush in.

'You shall not take them away! My girls . . . my babies! They are my only consolation!' I heard Mistress Dee call hysterically.

And then came the voice of her companion, placating and reassuring. 'Not if you don't want them to go, of course not! 'Tis a foolish plan and I will speak to Dr Dee about it. Rest easy in your mind, Madam!'

I tapped at the door and after a moment Mistress Allen, pink in the cheeks and with her head covering askew, answered it.

'I beg your pardon, but can I get you anything to soothe the mistress?' I asked. 'A chamomile drink, perhaps.'

'No,' she said in a harsh whisper, 'but you can take a message to Dr Dee!'

'Beth! Merryl!' I heard the mistress's voice call from within the silk coverings. 'My precious darlings.'

'The mistress has been much disturbed at the notion that her daughters are being taken from her. Tell Dr Dee that, if you will. Tell him that she says they cannot go, for then she will lose two more children!'

'Certainly, Madam,' I said, thinking that I would not and that she could do her own dirty work.

I ran down the stairs and tapped on the library door. A bad-tempered grumble came from within and I pushed open the door and looked through the smoke at Dr Dee. 'Mistress Allen's compliments, Sir, and would you please go upstairs, where she wishes to speak to you.'

As I said this another scream was heard and Dr Dee wearily got to his feet. 'Whatever is it?' I heard him mutter. 'What's happening now?'

Mr Kelly sighed heavily. 'Surely someone of your calibre and learning, Dee, should not be subject to petty domestic concerns?'

I said nothing, but went back into the kitchen, where I told the children that, unfortunately, they would not be coming back to London with me as their mother didn't wish to part with them. I tried to sound regretful about this.

I washed their hands and faces and sent them to their mother with the message that I would leave alone the following day, and also asked for money to buy provisions, the girls from the village still having not arrived. Once Beth and Merryl had been reconciled, blessed and cried over by their mother, the three of us set off for the market.

Walking through the familiar lanes to the village square I reflected that, in the same way that Dr Dee's house had at first impressed and overawed me, so had busy Mortlake when contrasted to my home village of Hazelgrove. Now, however, I compared Mortlake to London's tumultuous, noisy and smelly streets and reflected that *here* you could buy your provisions in a considered way, weighing up each purchase and deciding which of three stalls was the best for each vegetable.

In London, however, you were hassled, jostled and beleaguered to buy on every side and felt lucky if you got home with your basket intact and your purse uncut. Still, I knew where I'd rather be.

One of the reasons I'd wanted to go to market was that I hoped to see Isabelle, and sure enough she was there in her usual spot, with some tied posies of herbs on a wooden crate, exchanging gossip with the woman sitting beside her. She jumped up on seeing me and gave a mighty shout.

'You're back so soon!' she said, flinging her arms around me.

'I am, but not for long,' I said, returning her hug. 'I came on an errand for Dr Dee and have to return tomorrow.'

'But what is London like?'

'Beyond exciting! I've much to tell you.'

'And have you seen your sweetheart there?'

Because of the proximity of the girls I put on a mystified look at this. Isabelle, not realising, said, 'Lucy! Your sweetheart – the queen's fool.'

'*Tom-fool?*' Merryl, who'd been looking about the market for a stall with singing birds, suddenly turned and gazed at me with surprise. 'Your sweetheart is Tom-fool?'

'There!' Beth said. 'No one told us!'

'Shush!' I made a face of protest at Isabelle. 'He's not really my sweetheart . . .'

She winked at me. 'Oh no, he is not. Not at all.'

'Oh,' Beth cried. 'So *that's* why you didn't like the pretty lady with the velvet boots.'

'Hush!' I protested. 'You're talking nonsense. Tomas is not my sweetheart.'

'I shall ask him the next time I see him,' Beth said.

I took both her hands in mine and spoke to her seriously. 'Please do not,' I said. ''Tis but a joke between me and Isabelle.' I shot a look at my friend. 'Is it not?'

Isabelle nodded vehemently. ''Tis but our play-acting. Lucy has no sweetheart.'

Beth clapped her hands. 'Then we will find you someone here in Mortlake, and then you'll want to stay here with us.'

Isabelle nodded. 'That is very fitting, for today is St Valentine's Day. You must act as his messengers, and look about to find suitable beaux for the two of us.'

'But stay within sight,' I added.

The idea of finding us sweethearts was novel enough to occupy the girls for quite some time, during which I filled Isabelle in on all that I'd been doing: of my dressing as a boy, of my acting with the Queen's Players – which she admitted to be extreme jealous of, and my day as a stable hand at Whitehall Palace. I also told her of my several meetings with Tomas, though confessed that these had not really gone to my satisfaction because of Mistress Juliette.

In the end, however, I made myself stop babbling of these things, for I had so much to tell about all that I'd done it seemed as if my life had taken off, while hers had come to a full stop.

'But what of you?' I asked. 'Are your mother and family well? Do your brothers still work at the ostler's? How is business in Mortlake?'

''Tis poor,' she said, pulling a face. 'My brothers earn enough between them to put food on the table, but I find very little to sell at this time of the year. Matters will improve in May when the asparagus is full grown and the vegetables crop, but until then there's not much in the fields.' She indicated the posies. 'I hunt for fresh herbs to make these tussy-mussies, but because there's no plague at the moment . . .'

'For which we give thanks!' I put in superstitiously.

'For which we give thanks,' she echoed, 'people don't feel the need to buy bunches of herbs.'

'How about your other jobs: in the tavern, and being a funeral mute.'

She tutted. 'Do you know that no one really rich has died since the Walsingham boy!' she said, and sounded so outraged that we both giggled. 'I got a job for a few days clearing weeds from the asparagus fields, but because I couldn't manage to work the hours that the men did, they got rid of me.'

I pulled a sympathetic face and an idea was just beginning to form in my head – something I could do to help her – when I was distracted by the girls running back, looking very excited.

'You look so pleased that I think you must have

found us two sweethearts,' I said.

Isabelle laughed. 'Then may they both be young noblemen, with good fortunes and carriages of their own.'

''Tis not sweethearts we've found,' Beth answered.

'Then what?'

'It's the someone who came to the house asking for you, Lucy,' said Merryl.

'Asking for *me*?'

'The two village girls sent her on her way and said you didn't live here any more.'

'And we tried to go out and speak to her, but they wouldn't let us! They said she was just a vagrant and must go back to her own parish and not come round a-begging in ours.'

'But what did she want?'

'You,' Beth said. 'She wanted to speak to you.'

'But why didn't you tell me before?'

'We forgot,' said Beth.

'We would have remembered, but you haven't been back here very long,' put in Merryl.

'So where is this person now?' I asked, terribly curious.

'She is sitting by the milestone, selling gloves from a tray.'

'*Gloves!*' I exclaimed, for this word held a special significance for me.

By this time the girls, each holding a hand, were leading me through the market stalls.

'There she is, over there,' Beth said. 'She doesn't look too much like a beggar . . .'

But I was already running towards the figure with my arms outstretched, for it was my own dear mother.

Chapter Thirteen

'Sweetling!' cried my ma. 'At last! I knew that sooner or later I would find you.'

I clasped her tightly, conscious that not only Merryl, Beth and Isabelle, but also what seemed like a fair proportion of the market, were watching us with interest.

'How long have you been in Mortlake?' I asked, looking at her face and thinking that she looked far more careworn than the last time I'd seen her, though it had barely been five months since I'd left Hazelgrove.

'Not so very long. About a seven-night.'

'You just missed me, then, for Mistress Midge and I left for London some ten days past.' I looked down to the meagre stock on her tray and felt like crying, for she only had two pairs of gloves to sell, and they were of poor and thin leather. 'But what are you doing here, Ma? How have you been managing?'

155

She spoke slowly. 'I'm here because I'm homeless . . . because of your father.'

I nodded, for I might have known he'd be at the back of things; he with his gambling and drunkenness, bullying and bad tempers. 'What's he done now?' I asked, but as I waited for her to reply I suddenly had a vision of a pile of freshly dug earth in a churchyard, a small green bush of rosemary growing in it. I hesitated. 'He's dead, isn't he?'

There was a pause. 'He is,' she said, and – may God forgive me – I didn't feel a thing except relief. 'Dead and buried in the churchyard at home with nothing to mark his grave . . .'

'. . . but some rosemary for remembrance,' I finished.

She nodded. 'The feeling against him in the village is such that I didn't want to have his grave marked by his name on a cross, for fear people would despoil it. But how did you know?'

I just shrugged by way of answer and my ma understood, for of course she knew of my dreams and premonitions. 'How did his death happen?' I asked.

My mother glanced about her. 'I cannot tell you it all here.'

'Then where are you staying?'

'At the Harvest Home.'

'The tippling house?'

She nodded. 'I wash the pots for them and have a room there.'

I looked at her in dismay. 'What type of a room do you have?' I asked, for I knew the Harvest Home to be no more than a run-down tavern and gambling den, filled with men and common drabs who drank, gambled and fought the night away.

Ma answered in her usual making-the-best-of-things way. ''Tis a good enough place to rest my head. I tuck myself away under the stairs and sleep well enough.'

'A gambling den is not a very genteel place for a woman to live.'

Ma shrugged. ''Tis not too bad, and for sure I can handle a drunken man, for I've been used to doing so all my life.'

I hugged her again, glad that she was away from my father and yes, glad that he was dead. 'I'll come to the Harvest Home tonight, and we can speak more,' I promised.

I felt immensely weary by the time the girls and I got back to the magician's house and unpacked our provisions, for it seemed to me that I'd hardly stopped in the last twenty-four hours. To my surprise (for I'd hardly seen her out of the bedchambers before this) I found Mistress Allen in the kitchen, making a broth to try and tempt the mistress into eating. This was looking thin and unappetising, for she'd had very few ingredients to work with, but I was able to add a boiling fowl and some vegetables to the pot and by this knew it would last the family for at least two days. Longer, I thought, if that guzzle-belly Mr Kelly kept his nose out of the trough and went back to his own house to eat. I wondered aloud what he'd do when the Dee family moved to Whitehall (hoping I'd hear that he was remaining in Mortlake), but Beth informed me that he'd already secured lodgings for himself and his servant very close to the house in Green Lane. This was not good news, but was no more than I'd expected, for Dr Dee believed Mr Kelly brought information from the spirit world to the land of the living, and where one of them went, the other was not far behind.

Having settled the girls for the night I was just about to set off for the tavern when a handbell summoned me to the library. I went in, noting with pleasure that for once Mr Kelly was not around.

Dr Dee indicated a tower of books on his desk. 'See that you take these back to London with you, will you?'

Inwardly I groaned, for the pile was as high as a horse. 'Yes, Sir,' I said, 'although I will have to hire a handcart to convey them from the wharf.'

'Then do so,' he said brusquely. 'These are books that I need with me at all times.'

He made a gesture for me to go and I suddenly remembered the idea I'd had earlier. 'About the girls, about Miss Merryl and Miss Beth, Sir . . .'

He glanced up from the paper he was working on. Looking at it upside down, I could see a mathematical diagram of some sort, with a moon and sun depicted. 'Yes? What of them?'

'Excuse my forwardness in pointing it out, but I fear they are not being properly cared for at the moment. Mistress Allen is fully occupied with Milady, and the two village girls who were employed for kitchen work are not doing a proper job. Sometimes – so I've been told – they don't appear for work at all.'

He made an impatient gesture. 'Yes, yes. But your mistress won't allow them to go to London without her. Besides, they are still being tutored here twice a week by Mr Sylvester.'

'I beg your pardon, Sir,' I ventured boldly, 'but his tutoring them in French and numbers is not taking care of their well-being.'

I believe he would have liked to have dismissed me from the room for speaking so bold, but I knew that he *did* care about the welfare of all of his children – especially that of the baby, Arthur, whose astrological chart had predicted he would be a scryer when he was fully grown.

'But what can be done?' he asked.

'I have a friend in the village,' I said eagerly, 'a clean and hardworking girl who knows Beth and Merryl and is young enough to keep up with their merry ways. She is a good, plain cook and . . .'

'Let her come, then.'

I was so surprised I went on with my reasoning. '. . . she has sisters of her own and is well-schooled in running a home.'

'Yes, yes. I said, let her come. She must come in

every day until we go to London, and then she can move in and take care of the house and its contents.'

I looked at him, startled. 'I see,' I said, thinking that *this* job might better suit my ma.

'There have been several robberies in the great houses around here and I can't leave the rest of my books without someone living in to take care of things.'

'I am not sure my friend would stay . . .' I began, for I knew that Isabelle found the house exceeding creepy and would never, ever, submit to spend the night alone in it, no matter how much she was paid. Glancing around, I saw several sinister objects she might object to: the skull, the stuffed bird with its malevolent eye, the dangling ally-gators, the mysterious gold-banded box . . . As my eyes fell on this latter object I only just managed to hide a gasp of surprise, for the box, which was usually locked, was now *not*. Its padlock lay nearby, almost covered by the feathered end of a quill pen.

'Let her come here and I'll speak to her,' he said, making the impatient gesture of dismissal again, and I left him, my mind now occupied with the gold-banded box, which I knew held the show-stone and the dark mirror. When I'd looked into the stone before, I'd seen a most wondrous thing: I'd seen the future . . .

That evening, with Merryl and Beth safely a-bed, I walked through Mortlake village thinking about the show-stone. How I'd love to look again into its depths!

What would I see? Would it show that I was going to continue in the service of the queen? Would I discover if Tomas and I had a future together? Or might I get a glimpse of something I didn't want to see?

I heard the bellman call that it was eight of the clock. This was late for a maid to be walking out alone, and I drew several curious glances as, well-wrapped against the cold night and holding a candle-lantern aloft, I made my way towards the tavern. I walked swiftly, taking care to keep away from dark corners, for this was in an area of Mortlake set away from the river, with mean dwellings inhabited by beggars and pick-pockets.

I reached the Harvest Home safely, however, and pushed open the door. Inside I found two large rooms furnished with long trestle tables and a great quantity of stools, some of which were upturned on the floor. A poor fire glowed in the hearth and the floor was stamped earth, which had been puddled over with spilt ale (and probably worse) and smelled damp and unwholesome. Several men were already slumped on a table, seeming to be as drunk as lords, and another group were shouting in each other's faces even though they were but inches apart. A man sat on the end of one table playing a violin, while two or three women danced to his tune, weaving in and out of each other's raised arms and laughing immoderately.

It was not the sort of place you would wish your ma to be living or working in, and – seeing her before she saw me – I noted her hunched and nervous demeanour and saw her staggering away from someone who'd sent her on her way with a shove in the back. Watching her, my eyes filled with tears. She'd endured a life of misery with my father, and now, when he was dead and she might have expected to find a little peace, she had not done so. In fact, she was not now at the mercy of one drunken man, but of forty-and-one, and probably sixty-and-one on a Friday night.

I persuaded her to take a pause in her collecting of glasses and we went outside and sat on the low wall there. She began to tell me about the decline and death of my father, about how, before his heart had quite given out, he'd expressed sorrow for the sort of man he'd been and for the misery he'd caused in all our lives (for my sisters, too, had suffered at his hands). I heard what my ma said but I couldn't forgive him, nor, after a while, even sit to listen to her tales of how he was truly sorry.

'I can hear no more!' I said at length. 'I know it's your duty to speak up for him, Ma, but I shall never forgive him for all the things he's done to us over the years.'

'You mustn't speak ill of the dead, Lucy!'

'I'm not going to speak ill of him, in fact I'm not going to speak of him at all,' I declared. 'I undertake never to mention his name again, nor ever to refer to him as my father.'

She sighed. 'Poor girl! Has he truly blighted your life so much?'

I shook my head. 'No, he has not,' I said, for I didn't want her to bear the burden of thinking such a thing. I took her thin hands in mine and rubbed them to warm them, as she oft used to rub mine when I was a child. 'But let's speak of other things. Tell me of how my sisters fare, and my nieces and nephews, and give me all the gossip of Hazelgrove.'

She laughed a little. 'Why, hardly anything happens in Hazelgrove – you know that.'

'Then at least tell me why you're homeless; why Sir Reginald didn't allow you to stay on in our cottage for charity's sake after . . . after he died.'

'Sir Reginald may have been persuaded, but I didn't dare to ask, for the rent hadn't been paid for so many months that they were on the verge of making us go into the workhouse. Besides, Sir Reginald has not been himself lately, since he and Lady Ashe suffered the bereavement.'

'Bereavement? Who was it who died, then?' I asked, for I knew Lord and Lady Ashe had no children.

'Their niece,' Ma said. 'Lady Ashe doted on her and loved her as her own.'

'Their *niece*?' I asked, incredulous. *Juliette*? 'Are you sure?'

Ma nodded. 'Why are you so surprised?'

'Because . . . because her niece is at Court and I saw her only the other day, riding a horse and as fit as a flea.'

'Never!'

163

'Are you sure it was their *niece* and not a cousin or someone?'

'It was their niece,' Ma said firmly. 'The girl lived abroad – Italy, I believe – and was expected to make a prestigious foreign marriage. The whole village has been talking of it.'

'She lived abroad? Then perhaps they have many nieces...'

'They have seven nephews, but only one niece,' Ma said.

'And she died two weeks back?'

'Just before your father.'

'Do you know the girl's name?'

'I may have known it, but now I can't remember.' She shook her head slowly, then continued, 'Lord and Lady Ashe went to Italy for the funeral, and their house is even now draped about with black crêpe.'

I was lost in thought. I was quite sure Juliette had told me she was Lady Ashe's niece. Or had I misheard and it was another, similar name? Surely not...

Ma's hand smoothed my cheek. 'But how are you faring, my lass? You look fine and bonny enough – although your hair is as short as a boy's.'

'I'm managing well, Ma. I'm happy in London,' I said, knowing I didn't have the time to tell her about the company of actors, or of Tomas, or of my dressing as a boy.

'Is it not, then, as dissolute as people say?'

'It may be, in parts, but not where Mistress Midge

and I are living,' I replied. 'The house Dr Dee has taken lies close to Whitehall, where the queen's palace is.'

'All the same, I shall not think to follow you there, for they say the smell, disarray and noise are beyond bearing.'

A cry of 'Where's the pot-woman?' came from within the tavern and Ma looked nervously towards it. 'I must get back, Lucy. I don't want to lose my position here.'

''Tis a shabby place you've chosen to live,' I said, surveying the outside of the tavern.

''Tis not ideal. But I shall look around for something better.'

'I may have something to tell you tomorrow then. And you are sure that you don't wish to return to Hazelgrove?'

She smiled wryly, but shook her head. 'There I'm known as Drunk William's widow and people spit on the ground when they say his name. And you'll be back here in Mortlake before too long, will you not?'

I said I would (though in truth I didn't know) and, as another roar came from the tavern, bade her goodnight and promised to go and see her in the market place the following morning.

I called on Isabelle on my way home, and though she'd already retired to bed and was mighty surprised to see me at such a late hour, she was pleased with my news and readily agreed to take my place on a daily basis, looking after Beth and Merryl and doing a little cooking and cleaning for the rest of the family until they all went to London. As I'd thought, however, she said she wouldn't undertake to sleep at the house under any circumstances, especially once the family had left.

'Not with those critters – those ally-gators,' she said, 'and the dead birds stuck on branches – and those bones! No, you'll have to find someone else to bide the nights.'

I said I would, and moreover knew the very person.

It was probably near to eleven o'clock when I returned home and found the magician's house in darkness, and the fire in the kitchen almost out. I lit a candle and banked up the fire, then, hearing no sound at all from any of the downstairs rooms, tiptoed along the corridor and pressed my ear to the library door. The precious show-stone had been at the back of my mind the whole evening, even though I was sure that Dr Dee would have remembered to lock it up before he retired. I told myself he had done – but to no avail, for 'twas near impossible for someone as curious as I to pass up the chance of holding and perhaps looking into this most curious and strange object once more.

As no sound came from within the library and there was no light to be seen, I pushed the heavy door open. The candles in the wall sconces were out and the fire, which had been burning well when I'd been in the room earlier that evening, didn't show as much as a firefly glow, so it seemed that Dr Dee must have retired some time back. I turned so that the light from my candle fell across his desk and drew in my breath sharply. The box was there, and – perhaps due to Dr Dee's absent-mindedness – still without its padlock.

Seeing this I became extreme nervous – but did not allow that to stop me. Carefully I stood the candlestick down on the desk, reached towards the box and opened it. It was lined inside in deep-blue velvet and contained, as I already knew, the dark viewing mirror and the show-stone, that wonderful shiny sphere of smooth crystal.

My heart beat loudly in my ears as I reached for the stone and lifted it out, turning it slightly so that the light from the candle fell upon it. Looking into it I had the immediate impression that I was looking into a bottomless well . . . into air . . . into infinity. I stared until the edges of the ball blurred and seemed to rise to meet me, giving me the strange impression that I was sinking deeper and deeper into the crystal itself. As I stared, colours appeared within it, then shapes that folded in on themselves and stretched out again to become people. The shadowy figure of Tomas appeared and I strained to see more, but he began walking away into the distance and the globe darkened to show a poor and shabby room with a girl slumped on the floor within it. She wore a black skirt and red cloak, which was the only spot of colour in the room, but I couldn't see her features because she was bent over, weeping. I got the feeling she was friendless, lost and alone, and her grief was near overwhelming her.

It couldn't be me, I thought with relief, for I didn't have a red cloak. But who was it? Was it someone I cared about? Was it Juliette, perhaps, found out as an imposter?

I moved the stone slightly in a vain attempt to see the girl from a different angle and make out who she was. I think I may even have whispered, '*Who are you?*'

As I did so, however, to my horror there came a voice from the far end of the room. '*What?* Who's that?!' Dr Dee barked out. 'Who's there?'

Terrified, I slipped the stone back into its box and turned towards the voice. By the light of my candle, I could now see Dr Dee at the far end of the room. He was lying on a settle under the stained-glass window and looked as if he'd just woken.

I thank God that I did not falter in my demeanour. 'You startled me, Sir! Can I be of any assistance? Shall I make up the fire for you?' I gave a little nervous laugh (which was not in the least bit false). 'Finding everything in darkness, I thought the whole house a-bed. I came in here to make sure the fire was safely out.'

'I must have fallen asleep,' Dr Dee said grumpily.

'And all in the dark, Sir?'

'I prefer the darkness, for it's then that the spirits come.'

I made no comment on this, merely asked again if I should make up the fire, and upon him replying no, told him that I'd secured Isabelle's help in the house

168

and that she'd be arriving the following day to begin her duties.

'And she will stay in this house when we leave for Whitehall?' he asked.

I shook my head. 'If you will excuse her, Sir, she has commitments at home. She has to look after the younger ones at night while her mother works.'

Dr Dee muttered impatiently at these domestic details.

'But 'tis of no import, for I've found a trustworthy goodwife who has no responsibilities of her own. When you go to London, she'll be free to move in here at a moment's notice and stay as long as you wish her to.'

'Is she a responsible woman?'

'Indeed, Sir. As honest as the day is long. She will not only mind your house, she will care for it in your absence, polish the woodstuffs, scrub the floors and wash the linens if you wish it.' Dr Dee grunted, which I took to be assent, while I happily contemplated meeting my ma in the market the following morning and telling her of her new position.

He got to his feet and I handed him my candle to light him to bed, while I, my heart still pounding, went to bed in my own little chamber and thought over all the events of the day: my father dead, my ma found, two people employed, a girl who may not be who she said she was – and a strange vision in a glass sphere . . .

Chapter Fourteen

It was a fine, bright day, as befitted what was supposed to be the first day of spring. I'd been back in London for five days and, though I'd contrived to be around the palace on several occasions, had not set eyes on Tomas in all that time, nor received any message from him. I did, however, expect to see him that day, for I was in St James's Park with the Queen's Players, and we were to perform a new play, named *The Taming of the Shrew*, for the queen. I thought that Juliette would be accompanying the queen, and I hoped to get the chance to ask her once again about her sponsor. If she maintained it *was* Lady Ashe, then I would tell Tomas and see what he thought about it.

I was in the park because I'd remembered that Tomas had said the queen wanted to see a play acted as part of the spring celebrations, and by going to the Curtain and reacquainting myself with Mr James, I'd made sure I had a part in it. It was a very small role (for all the actors who usually played women had now returned to the company), and not one which called for me to be dressed in fine clothes with copious amounts of jewellery, as before, but merely to be a serving-woman in a tavern. I had to appear several times bearing tankards on a tray, and get my bottom pinched by a fat friar for my trouble.

I'd given some thought to what I'd seen in the show-stone, but the vision of that bare room and the feeling of overwhelming grief had been rather overshadowed in my mind by the horror of discovering that Dr Dee was in the library. If it was a true vision I'd seen, if it really predicted something which was going to happen, then I'd recognise it when the time came. As it didn't seem to have been me who'd been so devastated, however, I decided I wouldn't spend any time worrying about it.

I had, of course, acquainted Mistress Midge with all the happenings at Mortlake, told her of the two new servants I'd recruited and assured her that the mistress was making steady progress. We both of us knew that before the Dees arrived in London we'd have to find another home for Sonny, but so far had been unable to come up with any ideas. The ideal thing would be to get him apprenticed somewhere, to a blacksmith or carpenter or coffin-maker, for then he could live on the premises, but to obtain such an apprenticeship cost a tidy sum. Besides, a boy should usually show an aptitude for a particular trade and, though Sonny was ever-helpful, the only thing he showed a particular talent for was eating.

That day, however, I'd banished Sonny from my mind and was at the park early to put on my costume and concentrate on my part in the play, for even if I didn't have words to say, I had to act with the right temperament, and also smile and look outraged on cue. The play, I thought, was a strange one, and at the rehearsal two days before I'd judged it both confusing and brutal – and not near as funny as *The Country Husband*. Mr James had told us, however, that he was quite sure the queen would enjoy it immensely.

Before the play was acted there was much else for her to enjoy, for the palace chefs had prepared an outdoor feast and several different beasts (I recognised an ox, a boar and a sheep) were roasting on spits, being turned and basted by small boys. In a pavilion beyond these roasts was a gigantic display of seafoods: sturgeon, oysters, clams, lobsters and the like displayed in the most marvellous fashion amongst running waterfalls, sea-shells and pearls. To accommodate the queen's guests, five long tables had been covered in swathes of white linen and placed in an E-shape under the trees. At the centre of the top table stood the queen's throne, on the arm of which was her drinking glass, painted in gold leaf and encrusted with jewels. She also had a silver two-pronged fork, the latest fashionable table item from Italy.

I looked around, happy to be a part of this fair scene: the prettily domed pavilions, the candle-lamps ready to be lit, the flags and bunting on the trees, and the green bushes 'blooming' with pink and white silk flowers. There was a wooden floor for dancing, and even a fountain, which, it had been said, would flow with claret as dinner commenced.

While the players gathered in the costuming tent and the food was being prepared, Her Grace was a-hawking in the park, accompanied by some of her ladies and gentlemen – and I heard tell that her fool had gone too. This led to me wondering if he had Juliette on his horse beside him, and if they might be talking closely together, he with his arm about her to stop her falling off. How was I going to introduce the topic I must question her about? What would Tomas do when he knew?

'And how do you like the scene, young sir?' a voice behind me asked, and I looked around to see that Mistress Hunt had come out of the dressing tent.

''Tis a grand sight,' I said, 'and will be even grander when the queen arrives.'

'It will, indeed.' Mistress Hunt removed a pin from the cushion which hung on a chain around her waist and secured a ribband which had become loose on my bodice. I stood very still, breathing in, for although I was wearing the tight undergarment to flatten my shape, I always feared that the quick eyes of the wardrobe mistress might notice that I was a little fuller in figure than the rest of the players. 'I do not care over-much for this latest play,' she said in a low voice.

'Nor I!' I confessed.

'Though they think the queen will be pleased by it. I hope she will, for her heart is heavy, poor woman, and she needs something to amuse her.'

'Is she still upset because of the marriage of Robert Dudley?' I asked, eager for palace gossip.

Mistress Hunt shook her head. 'No, I speak of the latest plot by the Scottish queen. Gossip has it that the queen's ministers have had enough, for while Mary lives, they say their own heads are not safe. They are preparing Mary's death warrant and are to persuade Her Grace to sign it.'

'Indeed?' I said. 'But would she really kill her own cousin?'

'She must! For if she does not, *she* may be killed.'

I gasped and vowed, if I could, to ask Tomas later for news on this.

I walked as far as the 'theatre' where we'd be performing, which was a natural dip in the land, flat at one end and lined with benches bearing cushions at the other. Here I joined the rest of the players, stagehands and scene shifters, who were awaiting the queen's return. They were a genial bunch of boys and men, but I always found myself a little uneasy in their company. This was mostly because I feared they'd find me out as a girl by my voice and attitude (for instance, I could not forbear shuddering when Master Cutler allowed his pet spider to run over him), also because they were educated and quick of wit. Someone such as I, who'd had no schooling to speak of except for a few months at a dame school, was not able to converse easily with those who could deliver a quip or provoke mirth with a well-turned line. Sometimes I found myself laughing along with them without being able to tell the reason why.

There was a sudden fanfare of trumpets, telling us that Her Grace was approaching the glade, and all gathered there fell silent, straightened their backs and their outfits, and turned towards where the royal gentlemen-at-arms were lined up. A moment afterwards a tremendous cheer broke out as the queen rode into view on a light-grey palfrey with a falcon on her wrist, surrounded by a large group of jumping, yapping hounds. She was wearing a sage-green riding outfit, its jacket embroidered with flowers and leaves, and over her red hair wore a close-fitting net covered with tiny, sparkling stones. Behind Her Grace (here my heart gave a great leap) rode Tomas, dressed as Jack o' the Green in a silk cloak and hood, and behind him, in pretty matching outfits of cerise and green, rode the queen's ladies-in-waiting, with Juliette amongst them. Juliette, very much alive.

'God bless Your Grace!' came the calls from all assembled there: cook or courtier, musician or actor. 'Long life and happiness!' 'Long to reign over us!'

Such heartfelt cries always made my eyes fill with

tears, and I had to quickly blink these away before my fellow actors noticed such sentimentality. I then prepared to enjoy the day, for much would happen before the play was performed.

First the queen sat and took a refreshing cordial while a choir of children dressed in springtime colours of green, white and yellow sang a pretty air about the season's soft clouds and breezes. After this there was a display of dancing and a fair speech given by a lady dressed all in white, who crowned the queen with a coronet of flowers and called her Eliza, Queen of Shepherds, likening her ladies to milkmaids and shepherdesses. There was a pause in the entertainments while Her Grace ate heartily, then took her ease in a private tent accompanied by her ladies of the bedchamber. It was then that Tomas (accompanied by Juliette, alas) came to the players' tent to exchange a few words about that afternoon's production.

Of course, Tomas knew it was me straight away, for I was a female disguised as a male disguised as a female and in all truth I was not very different from the way I usually looked, although I was made up to look older and had been padded around the behind to appear fatter.

'I see you are playing the part of Mistress Midge!' Tomas said.

I laughed. 'I am certainly larger of beam than normal.' I curtseyed to him and then to Juliette, who nodded at me briefly.

'Here again, are you?' She looked around the tent. 'Is Mr Shakespeare here?' she asked. 'I have heard that this play is by him.'

I shook my head as I rose from my curtsey. 'I haven't heard that he's here today. I believe he resides in Warwickshire.'

Clearly disappointed, she began scanning the crowd for someone more illustrious to speak to. Her hair was braided very prettily, I noticed, and studded here and there with pearls.

'Are you well?' Tomas asked me.

'I am, I thank you.' I cleared my throat, wondering how to say what I had to. 'And are you and your family well, Madam?' I asked somewhat nervously, for of course it was not seemly for someone like me to ask a member of the nobility such a thing.

She gave me a sharp look. 'What an extraordinary question.'

I hesitated and blurted out, "Tis only that . . . that I think Lady Ashe a noble lady and hoped that all was well with her family. It *is* Lady Margaret Ashe who is your aunt, is it not?'

She raised her eyebrows. 'It is, and I'm sure she will be most grateful for your solicitous thoughts.'

I felt myself blush, partly because of the sarcasm in her voice – but mostly with shock. I had surely caught her out! She'd told me once again she was Lady Ashe's niece, but this was not possible.

Tomas looked at me curiously. 'Is something wrong,

Lucy? Are you nervous about the part you must play?'

I shook my head as one of the actors – a grand, over-bearing type – began speaking to Juliette of the great love he bore the queen.

I found my voice. 'Will you come to the table and take a glass of ale, Sir?' I asked Tomas.

He nodded and we walked the few steps out of her hearing. 'What is it? Why did you speak to Mistress Juliette so? Do you know her family?'

I nodded. 'Do you remember I told you that Lord and Lady Ashe own all the land in Hazelgrove?' I said. 'He is the lord of our manor; they are both very well loved.'

'I do remember it, now that you've reminded me,' Tomas said. 'And Mistress Juliette is their niece.'

'But that's just it – she isn't!' I said, speaking in a fierce whisper.

'What do you mean?'

'I had to go back to Mortlake last week and my mother was there, and she told me that Lady Ashe's niece had recently died abroad.'

Tomas was shaking his head before I'd even finished. 'Then the girl living abroad must have been another, different niece.'

'There is only one!'

'Then perhaps Mistress Juliette here is a young cousin or some other relation to the lady.'

I shook my head vehemently. 'No. Tomas, I've got a feeling about her. I think she's a counterfeit. She is no more Lady Ashe's niece than I am. She is merely playing a part. I am anxious –' and as the thought sprang to my mind, I spoke the words '– anxious for the safety of the queen!'

He burst out laughing. 'There are many who plot to harm Her Grace, but I don't think Mistress Juliette is one.' He picked up my hand and kissed it, looking at me playfully. 'Lucy – dear Mistress Lucy – can it be that you are as green as the clothing I wear today?'

I snatched my hand back. 'No, Sir! It's not jealousy that afflicts me.'

'Then I think some springtime sickness is upon you.'

'The only springtime sickness is on your part! The lady is false –' the feeling was strengthening as I spoke '– and the fact that you can't see this was probably caused by an over-indulgence in hearts, sonnets and flowers on St Valentine's Day!'

'But I was not at the palace that day.'

I found pleasure in this news, but did not wish to show it. ''Tis nothing to me, Sir, whether you were or no.'

'I had to go away unexpectedly for Her Grace.'

'Nevertheless, it appears to me that you are allowing your feelings for Mistress Juliette to get in the way of the truth.'

He shook his head. 'I merely think there must be another explanation.'

'Then for a while, we must agree to differ,' I said stiffly.

He touched my arm. 'I refuse to quarrel with you, Lucy. I'm the queen's fool, here to make people laugh. And today is the first day of spring and a cause for celebration.'

'In truth it is,' I agreed. I swallowed hard and managed to smile, for I didn't want him to see how hurt I was. 'But before you recommence your duties, Tomas, speak to me of the queen and how she fares. Someone told me that she has signed a certain death warrant . . .'

He nodded. 'She has been persuaded to do so, for 'tis certain that Mary of Scotland desires the English throne and will not rest until she gets it. She sealed her fate when she put her signature to a paper which called for Her Grace's death.'

'Truly?' I asked. 'It seems foolish to put such a thing in writing.'

'Indeed. Although Mary's supporters say that the words were added to an innocent letter *after* she'd signed it.'

'Then how does one know who to believe?' I asked.

'Exactly,' he said, raising an eyebrow, and I knew he was referring to the question I'd posed over Juliette, as well as that concerning the queen's cousin.

As far as I was concerned, however, there was no dilemma. My ma might be poor and old, but she could be trusted in what she said, and if she told me that

Lady Ashe's niece was dead, then dead she was, and this girl was an imposter.

Now I had merely to prove it.

Chapter Fifteen

'Was the queen looking well, and was she in good heart?' Mistress Midge asked the following day.

'She was. And she laughed very much at the play, even though I didn't think its intention was to be funny.'

'Who are we to judge what is funny and what is not when a *queen* is present?' said Mistress Midge. 'If she laughed, then the play was a merry one.'

I nodded and smiled, though my heart felt heavy. Tomas hadn't believed me! Tomas would rather believe a lady-in-waiting with long brown hair the colour of newly opened chestnuts.

'Did the queen have a suitor with her?' Mistress Midge wanted to know.

'She had several,' I said. I ticked off on my fingers, 'Sir Francis Drake, Sir Christopher Hatton and a

Spanish prince all wanted to sit beside her during the play, but they say she is not enamoured of any of them.'

'There!' Mistress Midge said with satisfaction. 'She's her own woman, that one. *She'll* never dance to a man's tune!'

'But the word is that she's accepted Drake's Diamond as a gift from Sir Francis,' I said, 'and all are talking of his generosity, for the stone is extremely rare – and worth a king's ransom!'

'Taking precious jewels is one thing,' said Mistress Midge, 'taking a man's hand in marriage quite another.'

'Was Mr James there?' Sonny wanted to know. 'He's a funny cove, he is. You could hide a badger in his beard.'

I laughed. 'Yes, he was there.'

'Well! Acting in plays! Whatever will you do next, Miss?' Mistress Midge asked. And on my shrugging my shoulders, added, 'Still, you may as well go off while you can, because when the master and mistress arrive, that'll be an end to all your jaunting.'

I sighed. 'I won't be acting with the Queen's Players for a good few days, because the whole company are removing to a house in Oxford to give some private performances.'

'Ah! Then you'll be able to help me sell sugar mice,' said Mistress Midge.

'I will, and gladly.' I nodded. Selling sugar mice would provide me with just the excuse I needed to go to Whitehall – and once there, I was going to brave all to try and discover the truth about Juliette.

The previous day the painters had finished in the room that would be Dr Dee's study (it was a tenth the size of his room in Mortlake, so couldn't really be called a library), and I spent the rest of that morning taking in his precious books and stacking them around the room as neatly as I could, ready for him to put on the new shelves as he pleased. The kitchen had already been cleared, scrubbed and had had shelves erected, and Mistress Midge was concentrating on putting this room to rights so that when the Dee family arrived the household would carry on as before: Mistress Midge would run the house and do the cooking, I would care for the children, and Mistresses Dee and Allen would shuffle about doing whatever it was they usually did to pass their days. As for Dr Dee and Mr Kelly, I presumed that as well as continuing their never-ending search for the philosopher's stone, they would offer a service for those London folk who wanted to have their dreams analysed, their horoscopes cast or their lost treasures hunted for, and perhaps there would be more customers than there had been at Mortlake.

After dinner Mistress Midge baked and sugared a deal of mice and, after helping her with the whiskers and noses, Sonny and I set off to Whitehall Palace with a batch of them on a tray. The open square was busy with people milling about in the hopes of catching a glimpse of the queen, and we marvelled greatly as a grandly dressed lady went past us borne on a litter, her bearers running at full tilt through the crowd, waving handbells. There were also many novelties to be seen that day: a dancing dog, a man eating fire and another carving a statue from a block of ice as well as the many ordinary street-sellers crying oysters, garlic, mousetraps or sugared rose petals.

'There seems to be almost as many sideshows here as at Bartholomew Fair,' I said to Sonny.

'Aye, there are, Missus,' he said. He was intent on what he called 'tidying' the tray of mice, which meant he would eat any mice which looked lopsided or uneven (and if there weren't any, would nibble one or two until they were).

'Sonny, I have a mind to get right inside the palace and see what I can see,' I said, drawing a gasp from him. If, I thought, I could discover where the ladies-in-waiting lodged, then it might be possible to get into Juliette's chamber and garner some evidence against her; some proof that she wasn't who she said she was.

'Go inside the palace!' Sonny looked at me, aghast. ''Tis said that curiosity killed the cat, Missus! By your leave, I'll not go with you.'

'No, you stay here,' I said, for I had no intention of getting him into danger and possibly taken back to Christ's Hospital. 'I'll leave you in the square to sell the rest of the mice. Can I trust you not to eat too many more?'

'No, you cannot,' he said stoutly. ''Tis too much temptation to put in the way of a growing lad.'

'Then I trust you not to eat more than six!' I gave him the tray – but took off two, which I wrapped in a fold of paper I had brought for just this purpose. 'Wait for me here in the square,' I told him. 'I'll be back before an hour is gone.'

'Suppose you don't ever come back?'

I assured him that I would, went across the square and through part of the coaching yard. I then did a very dainty curtsey to one of the guards standing in a doorway, held up my little package and said I was sister of one of the laundresses, named Barbara, and I'd brought her two gingerbread mice from home.

Yawning, he pointed me along a stone passageway and I went down this, passing through some open spaces, along narrow corridors and up and down steps. He didn't accompany me, so I was able to stop every so often to ask directions, and I also fixed some of the things I passed in my mind so that, if I had to, I'd be able to get out in a hurry. As I went along I observed a great number of people of all ages, shapes, sizes and professions, every one of them going about their duties and none paying the slightest attention to me.

After getting lost several times I found myself in the royal laundries, and arrived at a light and spacious pressing room, with piles of freshly ironed sheets and towels upon wooden pallets. These had sprigs of lavender scattered between the layers, imparting a sweet and delicate aroma to the air. There were several girls here either pressing garments or heating up irons on a range, also a most ingenious machine in which I observed bed and table linens being folded and pressed flat. Here I found Barbara in front of a window, examining some lace with a younger girl.

'Excuse me, are you Barbara?' I asked, although of course I knew full well who she was.

She didn't know me, however. Not as I was then. 'I am, it please you,' she said, looking at me curiously.

'Then I have something for you.' I held out my small offering. 'My brother bade me bring you these.'

She moved away from the window and peered inside the paper and then looked at me curiously. 'Do I know your brother?'

I took a deep breath, just like the one Mr James had instructed me to take before I went on to the stage. 'He's an actor with the Queen's Players and has also worked here in the stables as an ostler.'

She frowned, looking at me closely.

'He told me you were very nice to him, and might consent to do me a favour.'

Her face suddenly lightened. 'I see the resemblance now! Your brother's name is Luke, is it not?'

'It is.' I was lying and had been taught that to do so was wicked, but as I was only doing it to aid Her Grace, surely I might be forgiven, I thought.

She blushed pink, took my hand and led me into a little antechamber, saying, 'If I can help you, then I will.'

I took another breath. 'I cannot tell you all the details

of my undertaking, but first let me tell you that I mean no harm to the queen, nor to anyone who loves her.'

'This all sounds of some import,' she said curiously. 'What might the favour be?'

'I have to discover whether one who is close to the queen is a true friend to her or not.'

'You are a spy?!' she asked, suddenly excited.

'I'm not of Sir Francis Walsingham's band,' I said, smiling, but she looked so disappointed that I added, 'but I suppose I am a spy of a type.'

'And what do you want from me?'

'I don't want to incriminate you in any way,' I said, speaking very serious now, 'so I'm not going to tell you what is behind this request. I merely want to borrow a laundress's cap and apron, and to be told where I may find the bedchambers of the queen's ladies-in-waiting.' On her gasping, I added quickly, 'I promise you on my life that I mean no hurt or disrespect to anyone loyal to the queen!'

She asked in a whisper, 'Your brother was asking about Mistress Juliette. Is it her whom you seek?'

'It is.'

'I thought it was because he had a mind to woo her!'

I smiled. 'I can assure you that that was the last thing on his mind.'

'Then I'll help you. Our clean aprons and caps are kept there,' she said, pointing to a monstrously sized cupboard, 'and I have the very excuse for you, for some-time in the afternoon one of us has to go around the apartments of the ladies-in-waiting and change their washstand cloths.'

'Then today, by your leave, that can be me,' I said. 'And are you able to tell me where to find the room of the lady we have spoken of?'

Barbara shook her head. 'Telling you the way would be impossible, for there are hundreds of rooms here and you'd never find your way.' As my heart sank, she added, 'It would be best if I took you there myself.'

'I don't want to put you in any danger.'

'You won't,' she said. 'The guards are used to me and if I'm accompanying a new servant, they'll think nothing of it.'

I squeezed her hand. 'Thank you a hundredfold! If what I suspect is true, then those who are close to Her Grace may also thank you.'

'And your brother?' she asked, smiling.

I smiled back, though it jolted my conscience to do it. 'Of course,' I said. 'He too.'

Barbara tied my apron correctly, set my cap upon my head and piled my arms high with sheets and towels so that I could duck behind them if necessary. We set off briskly along the passageways, with me keeping to my plan to try and remember the way whenever possible. This was difficult, however, because the palace was beyond large, stretching in all directions and seeming to be the size of a village.

For three quarters of our journey along the passageways we were in the servants' quarters, with stone underfoot and the walls bare of all but rusty candle-holders and spots of damp and mould. When Barbara opened a door lined in green baize, however, we entered a higher realm, for here there were clean rushes on the floor and expensive Turkey carpets, and tapestries and painted canvases on the walls. The candleholders here were of brass, and the candles proper wax instead of cheap tallow.

'We are now in the quarters of the queen's ladies,' Barbara said, after going through several doors. 'A little further are the chambers of the maids of honour, and then the apartments of the queen. And here . . .' she said meaningfully, pointing in turn to three doors ahead of us '. . . are the rooms of Mistresses Penelope, Vivien and Juliette.'

I mouthed a silent thank you and said that she should go now.

'I will wait beyond the green door,' she whispered. 'Take care.'

I watched her retreat down the corridor. I knew I was on dangerous ground now; that if it was discovered that I was there under false pretences, being found in the quarters of the queen's ladies was probably a treasonable offence. Fearful as this thought was, however, I was sure in my own mind that Juliette was not who she claimed to be. If she posed a danger to the queen, then it was only right and proper that I should try to expose her.

It was, as far as I knew, about three o'clock, so the

ladies-in-waiting would be in the needlework room with the queen, or perhaps listening to a minstrel in one of the music rooms. I tapped at the first two doors. No reply came from either, so I went inside and changed each lady's washcloth from the pile I carried. I then tapped at the door to Juliette's chamber and, as before, there was no reply. I knocked again and, leaving the door open behind me, went in, my stomach a hollow of fear.

It was a small room, its walls prettily decorated with painted-on trellises bearing full-blown roses which looked so realistic that you could almost imagine you were standing in a garden. There was a four-poster bed draped in soft muslins, several velvet-covered stools and a line of hooks holding Juliette's gowns. There was a dressing table with a circular mirror in a wooden frame, a silver-topped hair comb and matching silver jar, a deep wooden jewellery box and a leather writing folder. There was also a painted washstand on which two towels hung. Neither looked as if it had been used, but I changed them nonetheless, for they were my reason for being there.

My eyes scanned across the room; *what was I looking for?*

Under my breath I cursed a little at my own rashness. Had I really expected Juliette to be careless enough to keep something in her room that could get her hanged? Walsingham and his spies were everywhere, so surely an enemy of the queen would not take any chances of being discovered.

I took two steps across the soft rug to the wooden box and, shifting the pile of towels to one arm, lifted the lid. This was a girl who loved jewellery, I knew, and to confirm this a huge array of jewels of different colours met my eyes: brooches, necklaces, bangles, rings and a tangle of pearls and gold chains. I was not an expert on such things but, at a glance, it didn't seem to me that any had great value, for if they had, surely they would be under lock and key, and not left in such disarray.

My eyes went past the box to the leather folder. I couldn't hope that she'd left anything obviously damning in there, but it might, perhaps, contain a secret compartment – and as soon as I'd satisfied myself on this point, I'd go. The whole undertaking had been dangerous and stupid. I'd have to find some other way of proving that Juliette wasn't Lady Ashe's niece.

I opened the folder. It contained several letters, but they were in Latin, that strange language that Dr Dee sometimes wrote in. They could have been incriminatory, but if they were there was no way of telling. Disappointed, I replaced them. And then, before I could look for any secret compartments, I heard a scream behind me.

'A thief! A thief in Mistress Juliette's room! Guards, come quickly!'

Chapter Sixteen

I thanked providence that I had the wit to keep turned away from whoever had shouted. I raised the pile of towels I carried so that my face was concealed, gave this person (a stout maidservant, I thought) a push to the shoulder that knocked her sideways on to the bed, then picked up my skirts and ran out of the door and down the corridor. The guards, luckily, were coming the other way, from the apartments of the queen. They had not yet turned the corner, but I could hear their footfall and the metallic clanking of their breastplates and halberds.

'Guards, quickly!' I heard shouted from Juliette's room. 'Catch her!'

I ran on and didn't stop to look behind me. After, perhaps, twenty paces, the corridor divided to right and left with, on the facing wall, a large Venetian mirror, possibly placed so that the ladies-in-waiting could check their appearance on the way to a Court gathering. I saw my reflection, a blur of white as I passed, then pounded on, exhibiting much more vigour than is seemly for a girl.

At the next corner the corridor divided again and I turned right, remembering correctly that I'd come past a large portrait of elderly clerical gentlemen. Here were more doors and, as the guards didn't seem to be gaining on me (for I could no longer hear their heavy progress along the corridors), I slowed slightly so that, if anyone appeared, I didn't appear a harum-scarum runaway. At the bottom of the next length of corridor I was relieved to see the green-backed door, and I went through this, pulling off my cap and undoing my apron as I did so.

I found Barbara waiting and was so pleased to see her that I flung my arm about her and kissed her cheek before hurrying along. (Such familiarity must have seemed odd to her, for she, of course, thought we'd only just become acquainted.)

'I fear I was discovered,' I said breathlessly. 'Will you show me to the quickest way out?'

She turned and looked at me, alarmed. 'You were *seen*?'

'Only by a maid – whom I am sure didn't see my face,' I said. 'And I think I must have shaken off the guards, for they no longer seem to be pursuing me.'

'The guards have given up?' she said, hurrying onwards. 'That's most odd, for they love a chase. They have been known to follow a mouse for a mile.'

'Perhaps they took a wrong turning and lost me.'

She shook her head, frowning, but did not say more. At a set of stone steps she took my apron and the pile of laundry. 'There's no need for you to come all the way back to the laundry rooms; if you go down here you'll eventually come to the palace brewhouse and then you can find your way out.'

'I am most gr—' I began, but she held up a hand to stop my speech and bade me go with all haste.

After some moments – following my nose – I found myself in the brewhouse. I thought it best to walk through briskly, as if I was on an errand, and so this is what I did, ignoring the men working there and passing through vaulted cellar after vaulted cellar containing malt, shovels, casks, barrels and all the paraphernalia for the making of ales, and every bit of the route suffused with the sickly smell of hops. Being made almost nauseous with this aroma I was more than happy to reach the outside yard, and when I did so, blinking in the sunlight, could not help a smile of relief crossing my face. Perhaps I'd not yet managed to catch out Juliette – but then I hadn't been caught out myself, either. I lived to try another day.

Walking briskly right around the palace yards, past tennis courts, a chapel and a line of shops built into a gatehouse, some minutes later I found myself close to the spot where I'd left Sonny. His tray was empty of mice now, and he was standing gazing anxiously at the door where I'd entered.

I touched him on the shoulder, making him jump mightily.

'God's teeth, Missus, I was thinking that I'd never see you again!' he said.

I sank down on a low wall nearby, waiting for my heart to stop pounding. 'But here I am, Sonny, and perfectly well, as you can see.'

'I thought: well, she's got in there but she's never goin' to get out!'

I was about to give a careless reply when there was a stir amongst the crowd, a murmuring and some movement, and I thought for a moment that the queen was riding in (for many of the people came every day with the sole desire of catching a glimpse of her). It was not Her Grace, however, but 'twas a grand sight all the same, for a lavishly equipped and plumed gentleman galloped into the square on a magnificent black stallion, accompanied by at least fifty gentlemen outriders, two by two in matching red livery.

The crowd buzzed with excitement and rumour. ''Tis the Earl of Shrewsbury on important official business,' we heard. And then, 'No, 'tis about Mary, Queen of Scots.' We also heard 'The Catholics are coming!' and 'The queen is preparing to go to war!'

Sonny and I watched the last of these riders disappear into the royal mews, then resumed our conversation.

'What's it like in there?' he asked. 'Is it all gold an' precious things, an' paintings and velvets an' jewels?'

I nodded. 'It is. Mostly.'

'Then 'tis not for the likes of you and me.'

'You may well be right.'

'An' you won't go a-nosying there again, will you, Missus?'

'I will not,' I said. And would not, either, tell Tomas of my little visit to the palace, for then I'd have to admit that I'd found nothing amiss in Juliette's room – which would be sure to lead him into saying that he'd told me as much. It might even make him feel protective of her, and this was not at all what I wanted. I'd have to think of some other way to catch her out.

We sat there for a few moments until my heartbeat returned to normal, and all the time I was keeping a watch on the doorways. No angry guards emerged, however, so they must have given up on me. Or maybe they'd presumed that I was merely a harmless soul who'd wanted to gawp at the rooms of the queen's ladies, and that to give me a scare was good enough.

The usual street-sellers and peddlers had sold their wares and packed up by the time we left the palace grounds, but two quack doctors had just set up a stall along the roadway outside and were doing a roaring trade in plague preventatives, for there had not been a really bad outbreak of the pestilence for the last six years and the astrologers were predicting one this summer. We looked at the cordials they were peddling and these seemed to be most unappetising and nauseous, being made of snail liquor, crushed beetles or the moss from a dead man's skull, and Sonny and I looked at these and agreed that, if it came to it, we would both rather take our chances with the plague.

We turned into Green Lane. 'Best not to tell Mistress Midge about my excursion,' I said to Sonny as we grew closer to our house.

He nodded, furrowing his brows. 'The fewer who knows, the better,' he said darkly.

The rest of the day passed in the usual manner, with Sonny and me playing a game of quoits in the yard and then Mistress Midge (in a very good mood because we'd sold a lot of mice) making us a fine and tasty pig's cheek soup with barley.

Having eaten and cleared supper, Mistress Midge and I settled to our mending, while Sonny sat himself on the front step and began whittling a whistle from a piece of wood. I was fine-stitching a petticoat and thinking over the tumultuous events of the day, when there came a piercing whistle from Sonny sitting in the doorway.

'He's made that whistle well enough!' Mistress Midge remarked.

Two more whistle-blasts came, sounding urgent, and then Sonny's face appeared round the door. 'Look sharp, Missus!' he hissed.

'*What?*' Mistress Midge and I said together.

'Lucy! Some guards are coming and it don't look good.'

I did not hesitate another moment, but jumped up, thrust my mending at Mistress Midge and ran out of the kitchen and straight into the room we'd decided would be Dr Dee's study. I'd thought to climb out of the window, but a new chair and oak coffer had recently been delivered and these stood before it, giving me the idea of hiding within the coffer. It bore a latch with padlock but this, fortunately, was hanging loose and I quickly opened the lid and slipped inside.

I found myself lying in a twisted and cramped position, my head pushed forward at an uncomfortable angle and my leg buckled beneath me, but was too frightened to move in case someone heard me. Mistress Midge came into the room and – from the scritch-scratching – I deduced that she'd realised where I was hiding, set the padlock into its holder and snapped it shut.

Several more whistles blasted out, as if Sonny was trying his new toy, and then I heard voices. Someone said clearly, 'Guard! This is where she dwells, I am sure of it. Search the place at once!'

My heart sank and I knew I was doomed, for the voice was Juliette's.

'Good evening, Madam . . . good Sirs,' I heard Mistress Midge say. 'May I help you?'

'This *is* the house of Dr Dee?' I heard Juliette ask.

'It's his London house,' Mistress Midge replied. 'Or will be.'

'And you have a girl named Lucy who is a nursemaid here, I believe.'

'We have. What is it that you want with her?'

'You'll be told that in good time,' a man's voice answered, and I pictured a large and objectionable palace guard waggling his finger at Mistress Midge. 'We want to know if the girl is here now.'

'She is not,' Mistress Midge said, and I blessed her, for although I didn't really think she would have given me away, she has a strange attitude towards authority, sometimes scoffing at the law and sometimes scrupulously obeying it to the letter. 'She has gone to Mortlake to collect some books for Dr Dee.'

'Enough,' I heard Juliette say. 'Of course you would cover for her. Which is the girl's room, old woman?'

I could almost feel the temperature drop in the house as Mistress Midge was addressed thus, and of course she didn't reply. I heard doors opening and closing and knew people were searching for me. Someone came into Dr Dee's study and I stayed as still as a corpse within its coffin.

'You were asked which was the girl's room,' came the impatient voice of the watch. 'If you are not going to cooperate then we'll take you with us instead.'

There was a moment's silence, then Mistress Midge said, 'Her room is at the top of the stairs. But what has she done?'

'She's stolen a quantity of jewellery from a member of the queen's household,' Juliette answered.

'By your leave,' said Mistress Midge, 'that is untrue, because she's been here all day with me, cooking and cleaning and getting things ready for our master's coming.'

Juliette gave a cold laugh. 'You are either deliberately lying, or have perhaps gone foolish in your old age. I saw her myself in my private apartments – glimpsed her in a mirror, running down the corridor with a handful of jewels.'

I had to bite my tongue to stop myself crying out. I'd thought myself so clever, slipping out of the apartments and getting away – but she'd seen me in the mirror! So why had she called the guards off and come round to search for me herself?

I found the answer to this a moment later. I heard dainty footsteps trip-trapping upwards, and after a moment heard her voice carrying triumphantly down the stairs, 'I've found my jewels! They were in her room!'

A shiver ran through me.

'Begging your pardon, but what have you found?' Mistress Midge asked.

'My stolen jewellery,' called Juliette, and I could picture her halfway down the stairs, holding out a handful of pearls and gold chains to show the members of the watch. 'They were on her washstand, plain for all to see.'

'I don't believe it!' Mistress Midge said.

'No more do I!' piped up Sonny.

'So, where is she now, Mistress?' a man's voice asked.

'I told you,' I heard Mistress Midge reply, 'gone to

Mortlake to take something to Dr Dee. She won't be back for days.'

'When she does come back, we'll be waiting,' the man's voice said. 'We'll come back in daylight tomorrow to do another search, and if we don't find her, then this house will be watched day and night. The moment she crosses the threshold she'll be arrested and taken to gaol.'

They left, and it seemed a very long time before Mistress Midge let me out of the coffer, by which time I was beginning to worry about whether there would be enough air in there for me to breathe. I was too frightened to call, however, in case the watch had left someone inside the house to try and catch me out.

At last I heard Mistress Midge go round the house closing all the shutters for the night and, having closed those in the study, come over to the coffer. She turned the key, opened the lid and held up a lighted candle. 'Come on, let's be having you,' she said.

I sat up and burst into tears.

'Cry quietly, mind,' she said, patting me on the head. 'And before you speak, I know you haven't done no robbing.'

Sonny appeared in the doorway. 'I told you not to go into the palace, Missus. I knew no good would come of it.'

I smiled through my tears; he only came as high as the door handle but he sounded just like my brother when he'd scolded me for scrumping apples from Lord

202

Ashe's orchard. 'I'll tell you what happened,' I began to say, but Mistress Midge held up her hand.

'Before you start, the less we know about it, the better – then even if they rack us we can't say a word.'

Sonny gave a frightened squeal.

I brushed the tears off my cheeks, and then began to rub my cramped limbs. 'Let me just say that it's all a lie, truly it is. I *was* in the room of the queen's lady who was here, but I did not steal her jewellery.'

'Maybe not,' Mistress Midge said. 'But why should she make up such a story?'

'Because she wants me out of the way. I know something about her, you see. She's not who she says she is.'

She shook her head slowly. 'I don't know how you've got yourself mixed up in all this, no more than I know how you're going to get yourself out of it.'

We contemplated my fate for some moments, and I wondered if Tomas knew that Juliette had brought the watch here to arrest me. Surely he couldn't have done or he would have stopped her – or come along to find out the truth for himself.

'First thing is, we need to get you out of the house,' Mistress Midge said. 'Those guards mean business. Come daylight they'll be all over the house like a rash.'

'There's a man out there now sitting under the tree in the moonlight,' Sonny volunteered.

'And is he watching the house?'

'He's faced in this direction,' Sonny said, 'but he keeps yawning.'

'That's good,' said Mistress Midge. 'Maybe he'll take a little nap.'

After an hour or two we couldn't see clearly enough to judge whether the man slept or not, so decided I should go out of the back door. Mistress Midge also said that it might be best if I left London for a while, at least until the fuss died down.

'And then you could come back here in disguise – in togs borrowed from the actors,' Sonny said. 'Maybe a bear's costume,' he added.

I sighed. I didn't know what to do. I didn't *want* to leave London, but had been made so scared by the day's events that I thought it would be a relief to be a way off. And it might only be for a short time, for if Juliette was an imposter – and she surely was – then the truth about her must be discovered soon.

'You can go to my sister at Syon Park,' said Mistress Midge. 'She'll give you a job in the kitchens and hide you away.'

'And I'll come with a message when it's safe for you to return,' Sonny added.

'But how will I find my way there?'

''Tis easy,' Mistress Midge said. 'Get out of the city a few miles – just in case, take a barge upriver and ask them to let you off in Chiswyck. When you get there, everyone knows the way to Syon.'

'I'll go with you if you like, Missus!' Sonny said. 'I'll go with you as your guard and companion.'

This idea was absurd, but strangely comforting, and so a while later Sonny and I set off with a hunk of bread, some cheese and a corked jug of small beer tied in a piece of old blanket. To further fool anyone who might be watching out for me, I'd changed into my boy's disguise, for they'd be looking for a girl on her own, not two lads travelling together.

We went out of the back door, crept stealthily through the courtyard and along the backs of the other houses in Green Lane. It was only when we'd gone some fair distance, however, that I realised that the city gates would be closed and that we wouldn't be able to get out until morning. And it was also then that, quite without warning, a wind blew up and it started to rain.

We continued towards Ludgate, thinking that we'd shelter near to there until first light, when they'd open the gates, but as the rain continued to stream down and the kennels in the centre of the lanes filled and churned with filth and muck, the adventure we'd embarked upon began to seem foolhardy.

Things became worse. First Sonny slipped near a slaughterhouse and fell into a stinking mire of pigs' entrails, and then I tripped on something dead and soft – a cat or dog, I thought – and fell badly, twisting my ankle.

I got up, tried to put weight on that foot and slipped over again. Cold, wet, tired and wretched, I began to cry.

Sonny took my hand, quite alarmed. 'Stir yourself to

move, Missus,' he said. 'We'll get taken in as vagrants if anyone comes by.'

'I don't care,' I said, and I sat where I'd fallen and put my head down on my knees. 'I can't go any further.'

'But we've hardly started. We're not even at Ludgate!'

I didn't reply, for I was feeling too sorry for myself. What was the point of going on? How could I hope to outwit someone like Juliette, who (whoever she turned out to be) was clearly of noble birth: educated, knowledgeable and well-connected? She held all the cards; what hope did I have of exposing her?

'Look,' Sonny said after a moment, 'if you can't go no further, then bide somewhere here. There's an old turkey pen down that lane . . .' He pointed into the darkness. 'When they drives 'em down from Norfolk they pack 'em in there overnight, afore the market.'

'I can't sleep in a turkey pen!'

'Why not? It's got a bit of a roof, and there's straw to cover yourself with. I slept there myself once when I ran away from Christ's Horspiddle. I was but a nipper, then.'

'Suppose there are turkeys there?'

'There are not,' he said, shaking his head, 'for yesterday was market day. Besides, Missus, you can't go back to the house, because of the guard.'

I sighed heavily.

''Tis but a little way off . . .'

Taking my silence for assent, he heaved me to my

feet. Leaning on him, I made my way up the cobbled street in the rain, trying to keep out of the flowing muck. We went down an alleyway, past old stalls (which, from the rank smell, usually held oxen) and came to a low, ramshackle shed with no windows and a sheet of tin in place of a door.

'Here it is!' said Sonny.

I almost began crying again on seeing it, for it was very squalid. Sonny, anxious that I should stay there, scraped up all the straw he could muster into a corner to make a mattress, and spread out the piece of blanket over this.

'I'll come back in the morning.'

'Make sure you're not seen.'

'Never fear. I'm an old hand at this, Missus. I'll come back with some food and a candle and a bit o' kindling to make you a fire. An' I'll get some rags to bind up your foot.'

I looked down at my ankle, which I could hardly see but which I could feel had already begun puffing up. 'Will you ask Mistress Midge if she has any sage and comfrey to help take down the swelling?'

He nodded. 'You'll be all right here, won't you?'

I nodded, trying to keep my tears under control.

'An' you won't run off?'

I gave a miserable snort of derision.

'And tomorrow we'll see what else we can do.'

I nodded and told him to go, for I felt I could no longer hold my emotions in check and I didn't want to distress him further. He went off and though I heard his footsteps retreating, I knew I was not alone, for the scuffling in the far corner told me there were rats. There were always rats.

I was in pain from my ankle now, and was cold and wet. I put the damp and stinking blanket around my shoulders in an effort to warm myself (which it did not) and knew that I had never felt more alone, or more wretched, in my life. Where was Tomas? Had Juliette managed to convince him that I was a thief? Had he, too, forsaken me?

Thinking this, I began to weep – and then stopped as I came to a sudden realisation. Of course! The torn red blanket I had around me was actually the 'jacket' that the figure had been wearing in Dr Dee's show-stone. And the figure I'd seen – bowed, miserable and completely alone – had been me . . .

Chapter Seventeen

I didn't sleep, and it wasn't long before I heard the watch calling five o'clock and, soon after this, cocks a-crowing, the milkmaids beginning their rounds of the streets, crying, 'Milk below, Mistress!', and the other noises of London waking. I would have dearly loved a pitcher of milk, for I thought it might restore me. I had only a few coins, however, and would need these, for in the time I'd been sitting around, shivering and miserable, I'd made a plan.

It gradually grew lighter, enabling me to see better the shack I found myself in, which was such a filthy mess of dead insects, puddles of dirt and turkey droppings that had I been able to see it clearly before, I'd never have suffered to stay there. I sat huddled in a corner on my grimy straw, not daring to move. Not only was I frightened of being seen, but I was also worried that, if I found another, cleaner hiding place, Sonny wouldn't know where to find me.

He came about nine o'clock with a shawl sent by Mistress Midge, an ointment made from sage and comfrey, a length of clean rag to use for a bandage and some more bread and cheese. Feeling pleased almost to the point of tears to see him, I flung my arms around him and kissed him heartily on both cheeks.

Alarmed, he quickly moved out of my embrace. 'Mistress Midge says you must apply the paste, then wet the bandage and tie it around your ankle as tightly as you can bear it,' he told me.

'I will,' I nodded. 'And is all quiet in Green Lane?'

'Apart from the guard outside,' he said. 'An' the ones who arrived at first light to search the house.'

'They did?' I gasped.

He nodded. 'Marched in two-be-two and went all over the house like they was looking for a priest in a whorehouse.' I looked at him, surprised at his language, and he added, shamefaced, 'Mistress Midge said that.'

'But of course they didn't find anything.'

He shook his head. 'They looked in that coffer, though. They would have discovered you for sure.'

'Then maybe I should be happy to have spent the night in this squalor,' I said. I picked up the ointment, unscrewed the lid and stirred it with my finger. 'But I have a mission for you.'

'What's that?' he asked suspiciously, all the time eyeing my bread and cheese.

'While I apply this I want you to go to the nearest

stationer and buy a quill, a bottle of ink and a piece of parchment.'

His voice took on a resigned tone. 'You're going to write a letter, ain't you? And I suppose once you've done that, then I'll have to take it somewhere.'

I nodded. 'Yes indeed. To Whitehall.'

'Then may the saints preserve me,' he said, sounding so droll it made me smile.

By the time he'd returned from the shop I'd wrapped up my ankle (which already felt better for being treated so kindly) and laid the red blanket on the floor in order to make a smooth area for the parchment. Kneeling down, with Sonny sitting beside me watching carefully as I formed the letters, I wrote the following:

For the eyes of Tomas, the Queen's Fool.

I find myself in difficult circumstances. If you value the friendship which we have shared, please do not believe what you may have heard.

The boy who bears this note will bring you to me, and I will explain all.

Yours always in deep loyalty to Her Grace the Queen.

Lucy.

I thought to send this to him with the groat I wore, as I'd done once before when I'd been in trouble, but when I reached about my neck to feel for the string on which it hung, I found to my horror that it wasn't there. Sonny and I searched all over the floor of the hovel, and I made him look outside in the alleyway, too, but it was not to be found. I was very cast down by this, for I'd had this token of the queen's image for many years.

I read through my written words again, reading them out to Sonny and worrying about whether I'd phrased things strongly enough. Had Juliette already spoken to Tomas and blackened my name? Would he really believe that I'd got into the palace to steal a handful of pretty baubles? He knew, surely, that such gee-gaws meant nothing to me. Once the ink was properly dry I folded the parchment carefully, regretting that I had no seal to make it secure.

'You must take this to the queen's fool,' I said to Sonny. 'And – this is most important – be sure that you give it into his own hands. He and he alone must receive it, even if you have to wait there overnight.'

He nodded earnestly. 'I shall do my best, Missus. But how am I to get into the palace in the first place?'

This, too, I'd already thought about in the dead of the night. 'You must say that you are sent by Mr James with a message from the Queen's Players. That will be good enough, for everyone at the palace knows that Tomas arranges Her Grace's entertainments.'

'Suppose I get caught?'

'There is nothing they can catch you for,' I said. 'You are merely delivering a letter.'

'Suppose they read it and see that it's not from Mr James?'

'The guards can't read! And even if they could, they

wouldn't dare read a letter addressed to the queen's own man!' I thought for a moment, then added, 'If you get into any difficulties, ask for Barbara, the laundress. Tell her you're my little brother, and she'll help.' *Poor Barbara*, I thought. When she'd flirted with Luke the actor, she little could have realised what she was getting herself into.

Sonny went off, somewhat reluctantly, and I settled myself to wait, trying to occupy the smallest possible space on the fetid floor. It was bound to be a long wait, I knew that, for Tomas might have gone elsewhere – to another of the royal palaces, perhaps on the queen's business. In the meantime I had nothing to do besides count the number of spiders on a spar of wood, ponder on the formation of cobwebs and worry about the trouble I was in.

Although cold and uncomfortable, I fell asleep twice, but was woken once by the street criers, and once by a snorting, grunting pig that came into the hovel looking for food. I ate the bread and cheese, more to keep myself occupied than from feeling any great hunger, and made a vulgar cleansing of my face by – oh, how glad I was that none of the elegant ladies at the palace could see me – spitting on a portion of shirt tail and rubbing it over my face. I then tidied my hair back, hoping that I did not look too far off neat and respectable, and entered a state of mind where just four words ran through my head: *will Tomas help me?*

First I thought yes, and then no. Firstly I believed

that because of all we'd shared, he would never let me down, then I thought he might; the evidence against me being too compelling. Forgetting I'd lost it, I often felt for my necklet. For long years it had been my lucky charm; was losing it a sign that things were not going to go well for me?

Hours went by and it was growing dark again when I at last heard footsteps and Sonny appeared, followed – how my heart leapt! – by Tomas. He was wearing a black velvet suit with a cloak lined in scarlet cloth, and looked extremely out of place in his surroundings.

'I got him!' Sonny said unnecessarily, grinning all over his face.

I struggled to get to my feet, imagining what a sight I must present to someone who'd come from the elegance and refinement of the palace. Tomas put out a hand to help me up, looking at me with such a mixture of expressions: exasperation, vexation, impatience and – yes, I believe perhaps a little tenderness, such as one might show to a pet that has done wrong.

'Mistress Lucy,' he said, giving a mock bow. 'Delighted to attend you at home.'

Being so happy to see him, I couldn't be cross with him for making fun of my predicament. 'How did Sonny find you?' I asked.

'He was riding through the square!' Sonny said. 'I saw him coming in this morning and recognised him.' A broad smile crossed his face. 'An' then he took me into the palace to wait a long time. I've been inside it!'

'I've been away for a day or two on an assignment for Her Grace,' Tomas said. 'Your young friend here was lucky enough to catch me as I returned.'

'He had to go and see the queen!' Sonny burst out. 'I gave him the letter, then waited in his room for ages while he went and saw the gracious queen Her Majesty!'

Tomas nodded. 'And during this time I was also informed by a certain lady-in-waiting of what had occurred in my absence.' There was a pause, then Tomas looked at me and shook his head. 'So . . . stealing jewels . . . what are we going to do with you, Mistress Lucy?'

'Really and truly I didn't!' I burst out. 'Can I just –'

'Before you start!' Sonny said. 'I don't want to hear no more than I oughta.'

'Wise fellow,' said Tomas. 'Why don't you wait for us in the street?'

There was a silence after he'd left, and Tomas looked at me rather sternly. 'I'll not mince words, Lucy,' he said. 'Directly after I received your letter from Sonny's hands, Mistress Juliette came to tell me that you were discovered in her room, and that you had stolen some gold and jewels. Do you deny this?'

I felt my face redden with anger. 'Yes, I do!'

'You were not there?'

'I was there,' I said, 'but I didn't take anything. Not a wisp, a feather nor a mote of dust!' I looked at him imploringly. 'You must believe me.'

'So why did you go into her chamber?'

I took a deep breath. 'Because of what I told you; what I discovered about her.'

He frowned deeply, but nodded at me to go on.

'I am perfectly sure that she is not who she says she is.'

Tomas was shaking his head almost before I'd finished. 'And I am perfectly sure that your Lady Ashe must have two nieces.'

'My mother assured me that she has not. The Ashes are the principal family in our village and my mother and the other village goodwives know their lineage as intimately as they know their own. Better, probably.'

'Hmm.' He frowned again and turned away from me slightly, enabling me to admire his profile and the shape of his nose.

'Don't you believe me?' I asked when I couldn't bear to wait a moment longer.

'I believe *you* believe it to be true,' he said, and after a pause added, 'and I also believe you to be innocent of theft.'

I sighed with relief.

'Could there possibly be two Lady Margaret Ashes? And could someone else have taken Mistress Juliette's jewels?'

'I was there when she said she found them in my room!'

Of a sudden he seemed to come to a decision, and took up my hand. 'We must go to the palace!'

'*What?*' I was horrified.

''Tis the only way. We must go to the palace, speak to Mistress Juliette and clear up this matter. We must hear what she has to say about it.'

'I cannot,' I said, shaking my head and backing away.

'You must,' he said. 'Or you will have a charge of treason on your head – for you must know that a violation against one of the queen's ladies is a violation against the queen herself.'

'No!' I protested.

'And if such a charge was brought, you and I would never be able to meet again.'

As I heard these words and understood them, my eyes filled with tears. I looked at him. 'Then I must go with you,' I said.

Chapter Eighteen

Tomas gave me the choice of going to the palace as I was, in my boy's garb, or going back to the house on Green Lane to change.

Vanity won the day, for I could no more have entered the palace and faced Juliette unkempt and dressed as a boy with torn hose and dirty knees, than I could have ridden on a hog to Bartholomew Fair. So, in spite of the seriousness of my situation, it was with the required amount of all-boys-together conviviality to fool the guard that the three of us went back towards the house.

Seeing him standing outside with his halberd I felt nervous as we approached, but he seemed more interested in chatting to a buxom street-seller who was crying fresh mackerel than in checking who was going in and out of the house.

I went through to the kitchen, surprising Mistress

Midge, who gave a scream when she saw me. 'Lucy!' she hissed. 'Lord above, what a risk to take! The guards have been all over the house turning things upside down, and are sure to return.'

'I had to come back here to change my clothes . . .'

'They even looked inside my skillets – though what they hoped to find *there* the Lord only knows.'

'Tomas says I must go to the palace to try and make things right,' I said, 'and I can't go looking like this.'

Only then did she look me up and down and take in my dishevelled appearance. 'No more you can,' she said. She pulled a horrified face. 'But – to go to the *palace*. Is that wise?'

Tomas appeared from the hall. 'It takes a fool like me to know that it *is* wise, Mistress Midge,' he said, bowing to her. 'I think Lucy must face her opponent, so that each can say their piece.' He clasped her hand and kissed it. 'I'm sure you agree, do you not?' he said, and smiled so winningly that Mistress Midge did no more than give him a simpering nod.

I went to the courtyard to draw some water, then washed my face, combed my hair and put on my best gown of green velvet, the one given to me by Charity Mucklow, the Puritan's daughter. It seemed, for good or ill, that things were coming to a head and I needed to look my best for whatever was going to happen. I was very scared, but knew myself to be honest and loyal to our queen, and determined that I would not be over-powered without a fair fight. Leaving the house, I took the same route as before: out of the house by the back door and through the courtyard, while Tomas went ahead and waited for me in Milk Street.

We began to walk towards Whitehall, each deep in our own thoughts. My ankle pained me somewhat, making me limp, but this was the smallest of my worries and I didn't even mention it. After all, I thought, a sprained ankle could be treated with herbs and simples, but a crime against a member of the queen's household was treated by putting you on the rack.

Tomas, seeming to sense my unease, began to tell me of the new banqueting hall the queen had erected in the gardens of the palace. It was, he said, made of white sailcloth fabric, lit by candle-holders and decorated with swags of fresh flowers. It looked exceedingly lovely and had much pleased the queen.

'And is Her Grace in good spirits?' I asked.

He gave a wry smile. 'Not really. At the moment her mind is much taken up with the problem of Mary of Scotland.'

'There is still much discord?'

'There will always be discord. And trouble, disorder, plots and counter-plots from those unhappy people who think our queen is not the rightful monarch.'

I went to touch my groat for luck when he said this, but of course it wasn't there.

'The queen has been talked into signing Mary's death warrant, but I fear she will tear it up at any moment. She doesn't seem to appreciate the danger she's in.'

Once this conversation was over we fell into another silence and, beginning to lose my earlier bravado, I started to fear the confrontation ahead. Would Juliette prove too clever for me? Who else did she have on her side? Was it just a scheme to remove me from London – because of my friendship with Tomas, perhaps – or was there more to her plotting? We went past a glove-maker's shop, which made me muse on home, and I wondered momentarily if Ma might possibly be wrong about Lady Ashe. Could she have muddled the facts? Just supposing, with the trauma of my father's death fresh upon her, she'd got the details wrong. Perhaps it was not a niece who had died, but a cousin, or godchild.

By the time we went through Holbein Gate and crossed the roadway towards the palace, I'd become deeply afraid and felt I could no longer trust my own memory. Suppose I'd somehow taken the jewellery without realising it? What if I'd placed a handful of shiny treasures in my pocket and carried them to my room? Was such a thing possible? At that moment, I feared the worst.

We entered the palace. I'd thought that every guard and parish constable in London might be looking out for me, but of course this was not the case, and Tomas (for they knew him, of course) and I passed through door after door without being apprehended. The deeper we went into the palace, however, the more nervous I became, until I felt such sickness and dread in my stomach that I felt I might vomit. For a pin, I thought, I would run out of there, go back to Hazelgrove and live in peace all on my own.

But I did not run, and soon we were in the apartments of the royal ladies. Here Tomas, asking a passing servant of their whereabouts, was told that a dancing master was in attendance in the music room and the queen and her ladies were all gone to be taught a new galliard. This, Tomas said to me, was always the queen's way of forgetting her troubles. 'She loves to dance – and is more sprightly on her feet than women half her age,' he told me, and though normally I would have been charmed by this insight, I could not take any pleasure in such things at that moment.

Tomas hesitated in the hallway outside Juliette's bedchamber, then recalled the servant and asked that a message be taken to her, requesting that she return there.

'You and I will wait for her within,' he said to me. 'Perhaps the three of us can talk quietly and have the whole thing settled without recourse elsewhere.' He took my hand and squeezed it, as if to give me courage. 'And then things can return to normal and we may go on as before.'

I looked at him bleakly and did not return the pressure of his hand, for I was afeared in my heart that we would *not* be going on as before, and that after today everything would change. I wanted to pause a moment and tell him this, but I could not for, believing Juliette to be in the music room, Tomas was already opening the door of her chamber and ushering me inside.

Thus it was that my enemy and I came face to face, and it would have been difficult to say which of us was the more shocked.

I stopped dead. I didn't believe in her any longer, thought her to be false, yet I'd been brought up to show respect to my betters and instinctively lowered my head and curtseyed.

'Juliette!' Tomas said. 'I've just sent you a message. I thought . . .' He stopped suddenly and looked to the bed, and I did the same. What we saw were several leather saddlebags filled to the brim with her gowns and petticoats, their frills and lace showing at each buckled opening. The room behind Juliette was almost bare: there was no jewellery box nor any of those little items that a lady might display on her dressing table. This lady, it was clear, was going away – although I knew the queen had no progress planned.

'You're leaving us?' Tomas asked. 'Does Her Grace know?'

She didn't reply.

'Or is this, perhaps, a private progress of your own?' I asked boldly. On her still not replying, I added, 'We've come here today to clear up various misunderstandings. And just in time, it seems.'

She smiled then, seemingly perfectly composed.

'Indeed. Do come in.' She ushered us further into her room and closed the door behind us.

'Lucy has the idea that you are not who you say you are,' said Tomas. 'I told her that she must be mistaken, but seeing this . . .'

I suddenly felt so angry that it overcame any predisposition to be respectful to my betters. 'I am *not* mistaken!' I said. 'I know that Lady Ashe's niece is dead, so you cannot be her! You are therefore false and no doubt an enemy to the queen. What's more, I did not steal your jewellery.'

There was a silence, then a strange smile spread across Juliette's face. I could not think why this was, but a second later became acquainted with the reason: someone had come silently through the adjoining door and was standing behind us. I immediately turned – but alas, too late, for this person had their arm tightly about my waist, and I felt the cold point of a knife at my throat.

'Do not move, or I assure you my maid will not hesitate to use that dagger,' Juliette said. 'We have not come this far to be stopped at the last moment.'

Tomas nodded slowly and thoughtfully. 'So, Lucy was right . . .'

'Yes, she was,' Juliette said, with a hard look at me. 'Once I knew of her role as your helper and found that she knew my aunt – my so-called aunt – then I knew I'd have to discredit her. As she managed to evade capture yesterday, I thought it was time that we left.

Especially as I have what I came for.'

I moved slightly, testing the grasp of whoever held me, and felt the point of the blade nick my skin. I couldn't see the woman, but had the feeling that it was the same burly maid who'd discovered me the previous day. 'Shall I tie her up, Madam?' I heard.

Juliette nodded. 'Tie them both up. Don't hesitate to use the knife on the girl if either of them make a move.'

She took two stools and placed them next to each other, then her maid pushed me down on to one and told Tomas to sit on the other so that we were back-to-back. Using a length of rope found in one of the panniers, they lashed us together, bolt upright and very tightly, so that the rope cut into my upper arms. Only then was the knife against my neck removed.

'The other ladies-in-waiting will be downstairs for perhaps two hours,' Juliette said, 'which will enable us to make our escape with some ease.'

'The queen will send armed men after you,' I burst out. 'The queen will . . .'

'*The queen!?*' Juliette interrupted. 'Do you mean that tawdry puppet who does naught but dance on the strings pulled by her ministers? That is no queen.'

I was shocked to silence.

'Madam,' Tomas said, 'I now perceive your true colours. You are a follower of the Scottish queen, are you not?'

'I am a follower of the *rightful* queen,' Juliette

corrected. 'The legitimate queen who follows the true religion.'

'And I presume you are set now for Fotheringay?' said Tomas.

'So we will know where to find you!' I cut in.

'I am able to disguise myself quite as well as you.'

'But you will never succeed in putting Mary of Scotland on the throne!' Tomas said.

'Do you not think so? Even now, her loyal soldiers are gathering to overthrow those who keep her prisoner.'

'But not *enough* soldiers . . .' said Tomas.

'Soon there will be many more.'

'I doubt that.'

'Do you?' She smiled, opened her jacket and pointed to a pocket sewn into the embroidered belt she wore. 'With what I have here, I can pay a hundred – nay, a thousand men!'

'So you've stolen money,' said Tomas. 'Is that why you came to Court?'

'I've stolen better than that,' she said with some pride, and it seemed she could not resist boasting of her feat, for she added, 'I have Drake's Diamond.'

'Never!' Tomas exclaimed, while I gasped in horror.

'Do you doubt me?' She reached into the pocket, brought out the stone and displayed it on her hand.

This made me gasp anew, for I had never seen such a beautiful thing in all my life. 'Twas about as big as a hen's egg and a deep, deep blue which flashed fire and rainbows where its facets caught the light.

'Lovely, is it not? And 'twas surprisingly easy to purloin.'

'But everyone knows of it,' I blurted out. 'You'll never be able to sell it.'

'No?' she said mockingly. 'How perceptive of you, dear Mistress Lucy.' She replaced the stone in her pocket. 'I have a skilled jeweller just ten miles outside London waiting to cut this diamond into forty smaller ones. 'Twill be a shame, for 'tis a very pretty thing but, as you cleverly pointed out, too recognisable by far.'

'Before you go,' I asked, 'why did you choose to take the identity of Lady Ashe's niece? Her of all others.'

She shrugged. '*Why?* You might as well ask why not. I chose her from a list of twenty young misses whose relatives were known to the queen but who were out of the country. One fly-witted girl is as good as any other!' She looked to her companion. 'Are you ready, Joan?'

The maid nodded, picked up two of the saddlebags, went to the door and looked outside.

Juliette paused, smiling down at me. 'And now, Mistress Lucy – so loyal to that whey-faced woman they call the Queen of England – I bid you farewell.'

I did not look up but stared at the floor, hating her with a deep passion.

'And Tomas. So devoted to the queen, so brave . . . and so willing to befriend a lady!' She bent down and I could not think what she might be doing, then saw her reflection in the mirror and realised that she was kissing Tomas. And he was not turning his head away from her!

They left, and as the door closed quietly behind them my eyes began to sting with tears. Whether this was because she had beaten us, or because Tomas hadn't evaded her kiss, however, I wasn't sure.

After a moment Tomas said, sounding almost matter of fact, 'They will have fast horses waiting and be on the turnpike road within ten minutes.'

I said nothing, knowing that my voice might give me away. *She had kissed him, and he had not objected!*

'She said they are set for Fotheringay, but I think it's more likely that they'll hide up somewhere beyond, some little village where no one will think of looking for them.' There was a pause, then he asked, 'Are you all right, Lucy? The ropes are not too tight around you?'

I composed myself, swallowed hard. 'I am well, thank you. Or as well as I might be when someone has implicated me in a robbery, hideously insulted our lady queen and stolen away with a diamond large enough to raise a thousand soldiers against her.'

'Ah,' he said, 'the world never ceases to surprise us, does it?'

I gave a frustrated cry. 'Are you not angry? How can you remain so calm?'

'I am the queen's fool,' he replied amiably. 'I must always present an agreeable demeanour.'

I wriggled on my stool, trying to wrench my hands out from the ropes. 'But we must get out! We must scream for help . . . have her stopped . . . prevent her getting away with that diamond!'

'Of course. All in good time.' I stopped wriggling, hardly able to believe his words. 'It won't be more than an hour before someone finds us. And in the meantime we can talk. But 'tis a great pity we are tied together back-to-back, don't you think?'

I said nothing, astonished.

'Have you any idea who Mistress Juliette really is?' he asked after a moment.

'Of course not!' I said. 'Have you?'

'I believe she may be the daughter of the Duke of Northumberland; the *Catholic* Duke of Northumberland, who – Walsingham tells me – is a secret supporter of the Scottish queen.'

'*What?* Do you know that for sure?'

'I was not sure, but am now convinced of it.'

'So when you brought me here today to confront her, why didn't you tell me what you knew?' I burst out. 'I was frightened almost to death that I might be thrown into gaol.'

'I'm sorry for that, Lucy, but I wanted you to behave perfectly naturally with her. I was not sure of my facts, and wished to know what she might do if confronted; if she would implicate someone else. Of course, I had no idea that we'd arrive just in time to see her escape!'

I was not happy with this explanation, nor the fact that he had not taken me into his confidence. 'But why aren't you in a hurry to go after her?'

'Because she can do no harm now. The enemy has shown her hand and she, her father and their accomplices will be picked up all in good time.'

I wished to be looking into his eyes for my next observation so that I could better discern the truth, but asked anyway, 'You must be sorry that Juliette turned out to be a traitor, for I think you and she reached a certain closeness while she was a lady-in-waiting.' I paused, trying to make my tone even. 'I believe she mentioned how willing you were to befriend a lady . . .'

'It is my job to befriend *all* the ladies.'

'Indeed. But with her, the befriending seemed of a special kind.' As I spoke I saw, in my mind's eye, their reflections, kissing.

'I can juggle, sing, turn somersaults and walk upon ropes, Lucy. I can also, when necessary, act the fine fellow, flirt and bend a knee to a lady.'

I swallowed. 'And were you still acting when you kissed her goodbye?'

He laughed. 'I believe it was *she* who kissed *me*! I am but a man, Lucy. If a pretty girl wants to press a kiss on my cheek, it would be ungallant to refuse.'

'On your *cheek*?'

'There only.'

I was silent, thinking about it.

'Lucy, I promise!' he said, sounding so sincere that I decided I would bestow upon him the benefit of the doubt.

'But what of the *diamond*?' I asked. 'She said that it would be at a jeweller's just . . .'

As I spoke, there came the sound of someone humming outside the door, and two seconds later it opened and Barbara came in with a pile of clean towels. 'God's teeth!' she gasped, dropping her towels. 'What's going on here?'

'Ah,' said Tomas with some joviality. 'Here you find two persons trussed like a pair of bantams for market!'

She peered around him to see me. 'Lord! It's you again, Miss! D'you want me to untie you?'

'I think that would be a very good idea,' said Tomas.

Barbara knelt on the floor and struggled for some moments, trying to unpick our fastenings, but the rope was thin and snaky and the knots pulled tight, causing her to swear several times under her breath.

'Perhaps you should ask one of the guards to come along with his dagger and cut us free,' said Tomas and, saying that was exactly what she would do, she shot me another wondering glance and went off.

'Before they return – what about the diamond?' I asked urgently. 'Do you know the jeweller that Juliette is bound for?'

'Alas, no.'

I gave a cry of despair. 'Then the diamond will be cut up, and each of the new stones will pay for a company of soldiers who will oppose our queen!'

'No, they will not.'

'What do you mean?'

'Just this: did you know that I was absent from Court last night?'

'I hoped you might have been,' I said, 'or I felt sure that you wouldn't have allowed Juliette to send the watch to Dr Dee's house.'

'I was in Salisbury. I was also there on St Valentine's Day, and so could not be the first lad you set eyes on that day and make you a present of a pair of gloves.'

I gave a gasp of surprise. So that's why he'd questioned me about the suitability of gloves as a gift.

'But don't you want to know why I was in Salisbury?'

Quickly recalling myself, I nodded.

'It was to visit the workshops of one of the most skilled craftsmen in the country. And yesterday I collected what he'd made.'

'Which was?'

'I think you can guess . . .'

'Tell me quickly, before the guard returns!' I begged.

'Very well. 'Twas a replica of Drake's Diamond, so like it in shape, weight and colour that Drake himself could not tell between the two of them.' He laughed. 'This fake was substituted for the real one, and then left as bait to see who might steal it, for Walsingham knew it would be irresistible. We hadn't thought that it might be snatched up so quickly, however!'

'So the one that Juliette is carrying so tenderly about her person . . .'

'Is made of glass, and will shatter into a thousand pieces if a jeweller tries to cut it!'

Chapter Nineteen

Barbara returned with the guard, who freed us in an instant, and Tomas went to seek an audience with Walsingham to tell him all that had occurred. Before he left, he arranged for someone to go ahead of me to the house on Green Lane and inform the guard there that his presence was no longer required.

Going back along the palace corridors with Barbara, I parried her questions as best I could and, as we parted, promised to give her best regards to my brother. I made a silent vow to myself to tell her the truth at the first opportunity: feeling infinitely weary by this time, I could not think of beginning the saga then. Yawning as I went, I walked back to the house on Green Lane and, after telling Mistress Midge and Sonny, in brief, all that had happened, climbed into bed and slept for near twelve hours.

I awoke to hear Sonny outside in the courtyard chopping wood for the kitchen fire and, quickly getting dressed, went to the kitchen and found Mistress Midge taking a new batch of mice out of the oven.

She informed me that a letter had arrived. 'I'm supposing it's for you,' she said, pointing to a folded parchment on the table. 'Someone wearing palace livery came with it at nine o'clock this morning.'

I seized the letter, which had my name writ large on the outside. 'Mistress Midge! You should have woken me.'

'We tried to,' she said tartly. 'Sonny tickled your toes and I dabbed your face with a wet sponge, but you were as dead as a side of mutton.'

I unfolded the letter and, with growing excitement, read it out to her:

'My dear Mistress Lucy,

Her Majesty has been informed of your actions in regard to a certain event, and would like to acknowledge your services to her with a small token of her appreciation. I therefore write to request your presence at Whitehall Palace tomorrow evening, when Her Majesty is hosting a gathering of friends loyal to the Crown.

I trust I shall have the pleasure of seeing you there.

Tomas.'

'Lord above!' Mistress Midge said as I finished. 'You do get yourself into some gallivantings. Back to the palace, eh? An' this time a-mixing with the gentry, if you please.'

'Indeed,' I said wonderingly. And moreover, *a small token of her appreciation*, whatever that meant.

Having been so late to rise, I went about my household duties diligently for the rest of the day, even undertaking that most hateful of jobs: scouring the sink with sand. Apart from this, my daily duties were not so very onerous and did not involve any deep thinking, which left me time to reflect on some most important questions concerning the evening ahead. Firstly, what form would this royal 'gathering of friends' take: would it be entertainment, dancing, feast or masque? I certainly hoped it would be something to do, or watch, rather than anything which involved having to make conversation with my elders and betters. Secondly, and even more importantly: what was I to wear? Seeing as the green velvet gown was a little grander than the pale blue, should I put this on again? Or should I try to add something extra to the blue – a sash or some lace – to make it more distinguished?

Mistress Midge, invited to share this dilemma, suggested that some artificial flowers might suit and brought out a grand old hat of hers with a spray of roses on the side. When we removed these and pinned them on to the blue dress, however, they merely made it look shabby – and the only sashes that either of us had were in such dull workaday colours that they did not enhance either gown. I therefore put the matter to one side, thinking that I might find the very thing: some feathers or a lace collar, on a peddler's tray at the morning market. But how should I dress my hair? The ladies of the Court wore an array of head coverings: little velvet caps, nets of pearls, feathers, stiffened hoods, coifs of linen spangled with silver – so anything might be put on one's head and not look out of place. Perhaps a wide ribband tied in a bow would suffice?

The next day dawned bright and looked like staying dry, which at least meant that I'd be able to walk to the palace without the hem of my gown getting covered in mud, and wouldn't need to wear clumsy pattens over my shoes. Completing all my duties at lightning speed, I sought Mistress Midge's permission to go to market and was just about to leave, Sonny beside me carrying my basket, when I glanced out of the window and saw, to my absolute horror and disbelief, Dr Dee at the other end of Green Lane!

I shrieked for Mistress Midge and she joined me at the window, where we saw Dr Dee walking slowly alongside a man pushing a handcart filled with boxes, rope-nets of books and small pieces of furniture, and, seated on top, Merryl and Beth. Craning my neck I could just see that this cart was followed by a plain horse-drawn carriage, which had Mr Kelly seated in the front beside the driver, and Mistresses Dee and Allen huddled behind.

'Lord preserve us!' Mistress Midge said. 'They must have come downriver on a wherry overnight!'

'But why didn't they warn us?'

'To try and catch us out, no doubt!' Mistress Midge gave a scream. 'We must put the house to rights, lay down fresh rushes, stock the larder, prepare dinner, make up the beds and beat the Turkey carpets!'

'What about me?' Sonny piped up, but neither of us took much notice.

'They've stopped at the other end of the lane,' Mistress Midge said. 'The girls are jumping down and going into a house.'

'Oh!' I exclaimed. 'They think the house is the other end of Green Lane.'

'What about me?' Sonny asked again. 'Where shall I hide?' We looked at him and gave sudden gasps as we remembered that we weren't supposed to have him there. 'I don't like that Mr Kelly,' he went on plaintively. 'He said he'd skin me alive if he ever saw me again.'

'Lord!' said Mistress Midge. 'What are we going to do with you, lad?'

I shook my head, worried, for we couldn't just push him out of the door and leave him to fare on his own. I looked out of the window again. 'Dr Dee is going inside the house now. That will give us a few moments' grace before they realise their mistake.'

'To do what, though?'

'To spirit Sonny away!' I said. I hadn't really had time to think through any of my ideas, so I'd just have to hope for the best. But before I began doing so . . .

I ran into my room and, leaving my blouse and loose

jacket intact, slipped out of my everyday kirtle, put on breeches and a flat cap and emerged as a boy. Then, bidding Mistress Midge to tell the Dee family that I'd gone shopping afar – to the poultry market at Leadenhall – Sonny and I left the house in the way which was fast becoming normal for me: out of the kitchen door and across the back courtyards.

Sonny pulled at my hand. 'You're not taking me back to Christ's Horspiddle!'

'No, I promise I'm not.'

'Where are we going, then?'

'Somewhere you like,' I said, for I was sure he did, and holding his hand tightly I pushed my way through the sunny squares, markets, dark back-alleys and slums of the city, to make our way to the Curtain Theatre at Shoreditch.

When we arrived the company were rehearsing, so we sat quietly at the side of the stage while Mr James entreated an assortment of sprites and spectres to 'flutter and fly, flap and float!' from one side of the stage to the other. As several of these ethereal beings were heavily built and considerably weightier on their feet than the real thing might have been, the sound of their pounding on the floorboards was similar to that of heavy horses. Mr James made them leap and twist in the air this way and that, however, wave their arms gracefully and endeavour to give the impression that they were flying, but it took some stretching of one's imagination for this illusion to be achieved.

This over, Mr James greeted me effusively, declaring that I had arrived just in time and could have a role that very evening. 'My dear boy, you are so slim and elegant of figure that you will make an excellent sprite!' He stood back and looked me up and down. 'Indeed, you must be queen of *all* the sprites!'

'I fear I cannot,' I said. 'My employer has newly arrived in London and I must return to my . . .' I stopped dead, for in the midst of all the excitement of the Dees' arrival, I'd forgotten that I was to attend the palace that evening. *How was I going to get out?*

'Then why have you come?'

'I . . . I wanted to ask if you would take on my brother as an apprentice,' I said, pushing Sonny forward.

Sonny looked at Mr James, awestruck, and then at me.

'He's a very good boy,' I said to Mr James. 'Most willing, and a hard worker. He can turn his hand to anything. Mistress Hunt likes him and I wondered if he could help with the costumes, or sell tickets, perhaps, or fetch and carry when you're performing outside.'

'But don't your parents need him at home?'

I'd thought of this. 'Father's dead,' I said truthfully, 'and Ma can't afford to keep him.'

'I suppose he can't read . . .'

I shook my head. 'But he's very quick to learn.'

'We do take on children sometimes,' Mr James said, walking round and round Sonny and looking him up and down. He lifted a strand of hair, seeking signs of infestation, and nodded approvingly when he found none. 'He seems a sturdy little chap.' I nodded, for Sonny had indeed grown quite rotund since coming to live with us. 'I hope he doesn't eat too much?'

I crossed my fingers behind my back. 'Hardly at all. He has the appetite of a shrew.'

He nodded. 'Good. Well, if he wants to learn our trade he's welcome to join us by day and bunk down at night with the other two youngsters under the stage.' He addressed Sonny, 'How would that suit you, lad?'

Sonny gave a deep bow from the waist, making me feel immensely proud of him. 'It would suit me very well indeed, my noble Sire!' he said grandly.

'Then you may take this young man to Mistress Hunt and leave him to her careful ministrations,' said Mr James, and I did this, promising Sonny that both Mistress Midge and I would visit often and bring him food – for he was concerned that, in view of what I'd said about his appetite, he wouldn't get enough to eat.

In the rush I'd not thought to take coins out with me but, not wanting to return home from the 'poultry market' empty-handed, went to a local poulterer I knew gave us credit, and took a fine Aylesbury duck to the house on Green Lane. Arriving back, I found a different Mistress Midge. Since we'd been in London with no one to oversee us I'd lived alongside an easy-going woman, but with the sudden arrival of the Dees, the old Midge – a scowling, harassed harridan – was back.

She had, however, thought to hide my kirtle and, as I peered around the back door, hissed at me to go to the privy and change before coming into the house. I did so, and also removed my cap, smoothed my hair and put aside my laddish swagger to assume a more maidenly aspect.

'Are they all well?' I asked in a whisper.

She grunted.

'Why did they give us no warning?'

'Just like I said: to try and catch us out,' said Mistress Midge. She was chopping vegetables and stopped to fan herself. 'I thank the Lord I wasn't seated outside, a-selling of my mice. And to think they could have found you up and acting with your players!' She frowned at me. 'But what have you done with Sonny?'

'That's just where I've taken him: to the players, where he's set to learn a trade upon the stage,' I told her. 'And I promised him that we'd visit as soon as we could.'

'Lord knows when *that* will be,' she said in a fierce whisper, 'for they've not stopped giving commands and issuing instructions in all the two hours they've been here. Their voices are ringing in my ears!'

'What shall I do about tonight?' I asked anxiously. 'How shall –' I stopped as Beth and Merryl suddenly hurtled into the room and flung their arms around me.

'Where were you? We've missed you! What have you been doing? Is it exciting living here?'

I hugged them back. 'It is,' I said. I paused for

reflection. 'Sometimes a little *too* exciting.'

Glancing past them into the hall I now saw what appeared to be the contents of the hand-cart tumbled on to the floor in an untidy heap, awaiting attention.

'You are to sleep in our room!' said Beth.

Merryl tugged at my hand. 'Yes, you're sleeping with us now! You must come and make up the beds.'

'Wait! Make up the bed in the mistress's chamber first!' Mistress Midge called. 'The poor lady has not travelled well and is sick. And then get fresh straw, stuff a mattress for Mr Kelly and put it in the blue room . . .'

I shot her an anguished look. 'Mr Kelly is staying *here*?'

She returned the same look. 'Unfortunately, his own lodgings are not yet ready.'

As she spoke the door to the study opened and the man himself appeared, wearing a stained travelling gown and looking disgruntled. 'Is the girl yet returned?' he called, then saw me and snorted. 'About time. Dr Dee and I are waiting for our books to be brought in.'

'Yes, Sir,' I murmured, and curtseyed in the slightest, most perfunctory manner possible.

Speaking to Merryl and Beth, I found that the girls had been well looked after by Isabelle, who'd not only cared for them and cooked for the family, but had also bawled out the two village girls when they'd eventually arrived, and made them return the several items of kitchen equipment that they'd stolen.

'We saw your mother again,' Beth said as I shook out bed linen. 'Isabelle told her that we were leaving for London, and she came round to speak to Papa.'

'She's living in our house now,' Merryl said, 'sleeping in your room!'

'Is she?' I said, and smiled with pleasure at the thought of Ma tucked into my own little bed at the magician's house. She'd sleep soundly there, I knew, for she was a sensible woman. She would not be troubled by skulls, bird corpses or floating ally-gators.

Mistress Midge and I did not stop working all day, but went from one job to the next, with much muttering, swearing and blaspheming on Mistress Midge's part and not a little on my own. We missed Sonny doing the heavy jobs: the chopping of firewood, the collecting of water and the sweeping of floors, and also discovered that the family had saved up all the tiresome tasks we hadn't been around to do in Mortlake and brought them to London for us. I didn't get a moment to go down to the local market for dress trimmings and, from supper time onwards, was in an agony of concern not only about how I was going to put on my finery (which I'd decided would have to be the green velvet), but how I was going to attend the palace at all. I found a moment to ask Mistress Midge's advice, and was answered by her throwing her apron over her head and calling down a plague upon me for giving her more problems.

After supper that evening, the house settled a little. Dr Dee and Mr Kelly were in the study, Milady and Mistress Allen were upstairs conversing in low and serious tones (for I could hear their murmurs through the floorboards), while I sat with Beth and Merryl, uneasily telling them stories of when I was a girl in the country while listening to the watch mark the hours.

At seven of the clock I knew *something* must be done. Darkness had fallen, but it was still too early for the three of us to retire to bed – and anyway, as I was sleeping with the girls I couldn't hope to escape until they were fast asleep. *And* I had to put on my best gown, for I could hardly appear before the queen and Court in my grease-spotted kirtle. I paced about, chewed my lip, tried to remember the tale I was supposed to be telling and paced about some more. I had to get out of the house. *I had to . . .*

'Shall we play dressing up?' I asked the girls in sudden desperation.

'Dressing up . . .' Merryl repeated curiously. 'What is that?'

'It's just a game,' I said. 'Like blind man's buff or ducking apples. The actors in plays do it. You have to dress as . . . as different people.'

'But I hate being pinned and unpinned,' Merryl said.

'Then *I'll* dress up,' I said. 'I'll put on my best gown and you can try and guess who I'm supposed to be.'

'I still can't see why,' Beth said.

'But if you wish,' her sister added politely.

We went to our bedchamber and I took the green velvet gown out of its box and endeavoured to shake out its creases. Beth and Merryl sat on their bed, staring, bewildered, as I first pinned the sleeves on to the bodice, then stepped into the petticoats and kirtle and fastened them around me. Pinned to my satisfaction, I walked up and down a little (for my ankle had improved greatly from Mistress Midge's herbal remedy and now hardly pained me at all).

'This is my finest gown,' I said to the girls. 'What do you think? Do I look like a nursemaid, or do I look like a lady at Court?'

Beth frowned. 'Well, a *little* bit like a lady . . .'

I took a ribband, fashioned it into a bow and fastened it into my hair. 'Now, does this look very fine?'

'*Quite* fine,' Beth said, head on one side.

'You need some jewels to be a real lady!' Merryl said suddenly. 'And an embroidered bolero and a feathered fan. And satin shoes and a pomander on a chain.'

I shrugged, suddenly feeling despondent. 'Those things I do not possess.'

'Well, never mind,' Beth said, 'because you *are* only a maid.'

'What happens when you play this dressing up?' Merryl asked. 'When do you change back to yourself again?'

'Oh, a bit later,' I said. Stomach churning, I wondered exactly what the hour was, and at what time

I was supposed to be at the palace, for Tomas hadn't thought to inform me of this. Oh, why was everything such a mess and a muddle?

Suddenly, the handbell rang from the study.

'Papa wants something,' Beth said.

I took off my hair decoration and went through to the hall to find Mr Kelly shaking the handbell for the second time. From within the study I heard Dr Dee's voice chanting something – one strange, foreign-sounding word – over and over.

'Quickly, quickly! Our fire is almost out!' Mr Kelly said, not seeming to notice I was in all my finery. 'It seems you have been growing negligent in these weeks out of your master's sight.'

I curtseyed and murmured something which might have been *Sorry, Sir*, but was actually an impolite expression I'd heard one of the watermen use.

'Come on, girl!' he said, clapping his hands.

I turned to go and get wood from the kitchen, but at that moment there was a knock on the door.

'Answer that,' said Mr Kelly, although he was standing right beside it.

The chanting from Dr Dee stopped. 'Quickly with the firewood,' he called from within. ''Tis damned cold in here.'

I hesitated a moment, then opened the front door to discover – to my enormous surprise – a man wearing the royal colours and a livery badge. Mr Kelly saw him at the same time and elbowed me out of the way, bowing and asking in a fawning way if he might be of service.

'I have instructions to bring a Mistress Lucy to the palace,' the man said, while I stood, amazed and immobile.

'There is not . . .' Mr Kelly began, then looked at me and his jaw dropped. '*What?* What has she done?'

'I have instructions to convey her hence,' the man said.

Dr Dee appeared. 'What is it? Does the queen want me?'

'I fear not, Sire,' the carrier said. 'I come for Mistress Lucy.'

I suddenly found the means to speak. 'I am Mistress Lucy.'

'Then, Madam, may we proceed?' said the carrier.

'Of course,' I said grandly, and without more ado stepped under Mr Kelly's arm, curtseyed to my employer, then climbed on to the litter (one bearer at the front, two at the back) which had been placed on the cobbles. I had a wool rug tucked around me and two cushions were placed at my back.

'Aloft!' the bearer called, and I felt myself lifted rather unsteadily into the air.

I glanced back at the house, gave my girls (now at the door also) a goodbye wave, and felt myself propelled forwards at some speed.

I lacked a fancy hat and had neither satin shoes, pomander nor fashionable outfit – but nevertheless, was on my way to the palace . . .

Chapter Twenty

I would, I decided, concern myself later about what Dr Dee and Mr Kelly might have to say regarding my being collected by a royal litter, for I was so very excited by what had happened, so full of anticipation, that I did not want to think on anything which might spoil the occasion. The curtains on my litter were open, so I sat back and, once used to the unsteady motion, enjoyed my new elevated aspect, the indoor scenes viewed through undraped windows and the envious glances of those we passed on foot. As we neared the Strand the houses grew more stately, with countless candles lit within, and I could scarcely take in their costly interiors, their tapestries, paintings and polished furniture quickly enough.

Entering the square which fronted the palace (ablaze with light, with much happening and many people coming and going) the litter-bearer deposited me at the fountain, where waited Tomas. He was dressed in what, for him, must have been conventional mode: as court jester, wearing a patchwork coat with bells along the hem and at the elbows, and breeches having one leg of green and one of red. His deep hood extended into a cape over his shoulders and this too was decorated with bells, so that a-jingling and a-jangling accompanied his every movement.

The bearers lowered my litter to the floor and I stepped out, whereupon Tomas smiled, bowed over my hand and kissed it as if I were a lady.

'I thank you kindly,' I said. I gave a low curtsey, now wishing most desperately that I'd been able to wear a gown which was more costly, more fashionable, more *enticing* than this, which I'd worn a dozen times before. But Tomas did not seem to notice my gown, and indeed was smiling at me very warmly indeed.

'Did you enjoy your journey?' he asked.

'Very much! 'Tis the first time I've travelled so. But mostly, before we set out, I enjoyed seeing the face of Mr Kelly when he realised that the litter was meant for me!'

Tomas laughed and offered me his arm, and we began to walk across the square. 'I realised I'd given you neither time nor destination,' he said, 'so thought it appropriate to send for you.'

'Then I'm very much obliged for your consideration.'

These little formalities over, I asked of the where-abouts of Mistress Juliette and whether or not she'd been apprehended. I was told that she had not – not yet.

'Then might she still be a danger to the queen?' I asked somewhat anxiously.

'Nay! She is a marked woman.' Tomas was carrying a jester's stick with a doll-head at the end and waved it aloft, bells jangling. 'She has as much power as this poppet!'

Satisfied with this, I sought to find out more about the evening ahead, asking him what might happen and what was its purpose.

''Tis merely one of the entertainments that the queen so loves to give from time to time,' he answered with a shrug. 'Mostly these are held to impress her foreign suitors and visiting ambassadors. There are many such in England at the moment.'

'And what form will the evening take?'

'There will be some dancing by the maids of honour, and a masque and some other diversions – including a fire-eater and fireworks at the festivities' end.'

I gasped, delighted.

'At some stage I believe the queen will ask to meet you – and I believe may present you with a mark of her appreciation.'

I stopped walking, all the more to savour the notion that I was to be presented to the queen. 'What sort of a mark?' I could not resist asking.

He shrugged. 'Perhaps a ring or brooch bearing her

insignia. Mayhap it will replace the lost groat in your affections.'

'Oh, it will!' I said, and fell into a happy reverie about wearing this pretty piece of jewellery and, on it being admired, being able to give its provenance.

We walked on, but did not proceed into the palace itself, but went through the orchard and across the tilt yard. Ahead of us was a vast edifice of white canvas and silvery oak attached to a palace wall. I was very amazed at seeing it, for the material was such that the whole structure seemed to glow from within.

'Is *this* the new banqueting hall?' I asked.

Tomas nodded. ''Twas built to remain just a few months, but the queen is so enamoured of it that I believe it may stay longer.'

We entered and I saw that the exterior glow came from the many burners, torches and candles placed within which gleamed through the fabric. Grasses and herbs grew underfoot and these, being bruised as they were walked upon, released their fragrance into the air. There were living trees within the structure, vast swags of sweet-smelling flowers intermixed with green vines, and vases containing branches of pink and white blossom, so that the whole effect was one of extreme beauty.

''Tis all most wonderful!' I said, gazing about me. 'And difficult to know whether we are inside or out.'

Tomas nodded. 'That is just what the queen wanted.'

To one side of the hall, long tables had been erected, and these were filled with all manner of sweetmeats in glass and silver dishes. On the centre table stood the queen's arms in sugarwork and, displayed beneath, spun-sugar nests filled with nuts and fruit, crystallised rose petals and frosted herb leaves. Each of the other tables was headed by one of the queen's beasts, also in sugarwork, and spun nests filled with a different form of confectionery: marchpane cakes, jellies, fruit in aspic, orange suckets, cinnamon comfits and the like. I could have stood there for an age staring at this display of wonders, for every type of delightful confection was there.

At one end of the structure some musicians were playing and a small stage had been erected. This was fronted by three rows of seats and a gilded throne. Looking about, I realised I need not have worried about the comparative drabness of my gown, for those assembled there took not the slightest notice of me. Some people acknowledged Tomas with a nod, but then, their eyes passing on to see who accompanied him, slid over me and away, as if they could discern immediately that I was a nobody. If only, the thought suddenly hit me, I'd had the wit to ask Mistress Hunt if I could borrow the gown of Mistress Mistletoe! *Then* I might have merited more than a cursory glance.

Tomas came and went from my side as his various responsibilities dictated, but I didn't mind this in the least, for being in the background gave me leave to gaze on and marvel at the variety of the exquisite gowns around me. I saw gold, magenta, scarlet, ivory, azure, vermilion and daffy-dill yellow at a glance, and sapphire, jade, lilac, silver and petal-pink at another – and all these gowns bejewelled and embroidered to the most marvellous degree. The gentlemen were no less finely clad, and these glittering creatures approached and greeted each other effusively, with much bowing and curtseying, fan-fluttering and hat-flourishing, like wonderful butterflies or other exotic specimens of nature.

When the hall was full of people the Lord Chamberlain came upon the stage and asked those gathered to prepare to take the blessing of their sovereign lady Queen Elizabeth, which caused a great stir and made us, as one, sink into our deepest curtseys or bow very low from the waist. A fanfare of trumpets sounded and an instant later I knew that Her Grace had entered the hall, for the very air about us became charged and vibrant.

The queen was accompanied by a body of finely dressed courtiers, and as she walked she blessed those she passed, smiling to each side and greeting those recognised by her. As she moved through a section of the hall, the people there rose and began to cheer and applaud, so that by the time she took her throne at the front of the stage the whole place was ringing with the heartfelt approbation of her subjects. This not dying down, she rose from her seat and, taking to the stage, thanked us all heartily, saying, 'The well-being of my people is the chiefest thing in the world that I do pray for', which made everyone cheer anew. I now moved to take a better position from which to see her and admire her gown. This was the most wonderful creation of silver and white tulle, with an immense ruff of silver lace spread like wings behind her head, decorated with rubies hanging as thickly as cherries from a tree in spring.

The audience becoming quiet, she regained her seat before the stage, and the courtiers she'd arrived with sat down. A small masque commenced, which – now that I'd seen for myself the cleverness and sophistication of the Queen's Players – I fear did not hold my attention greatly. While this was playing, therefore, I amused myself by discerning numerous flirtations between the elegant ladies and distinguished gentlemen around me.

When the masque finished, there was a display of country dancing by children, and then a pretty dance with ribbands given by some of the Court ladies, who stepped and twisted in and out of each other to make a pattern with their differently coloured strands. It was after this, Tomas had already informed me, that the queen was firstly going to take refreshment from the displays of sweetmeats, and then walk about the hall meeting some of her people – myself included. I began to feel nervous, wondering what she might say to me and what I would reply.

The dance ended, the music ceased – and just at that split second of silence, where one has to make quite sure that everything has really come to a close before applauding – there came sounds outside of horses galloping and being reined in, followed by some shouts from the queen's guards. Applause for the dance began but was half-hearted, for everyone was wondering what had caused the disturbance. An instant later we found it out, for the canvas doors swung open and a black-coated messenger ran in: hatless, breathless, his face and clothes spattered with mud. Two of the gentlemen closest to the door seemed to protest at this intrusion and rose as if they would catch hold of him, but, evading them, he ran to the queen and knelt low before her, holding up a rolled parchment.

The hall was now absolutely silent and every eye was on the queen. I glanced at Tomas standing at the side of the stage, his jester's colours giving the lie to his pallid face. The queen took off the seal, unrolled the parchment and, frowning, read what was written there. She gave a loud scream (of fury, some said, while others said of fear) and immediately hurried from the hall, followed at once by her maids of honour and some of the gentlemen.

She left behind consternation and anxiety, and rumours began to run through the hall like a summer fire over a heath: war has been declared on us by France . . . by Spain . . . by the Low Countries; a great plague is on its way; a comet has been seen in the sky foretelling fire; Hampton Court Palace has burned to the ground . . .

The messenger (whom the queen had left prostrate on the floor) picked himself up and was immediately seized by those of the queen's councillors who'd stayed behind. Two of his riding companions entered, and were similarly taken. A few moments later, someone (I did not know his name, but took him to be a dignitary by his chains of office) stepped on to the low stage and lifted his hands for silence. The hall was at peace within seconds.

'Her Grace has been very much disturbed by some news that has just arrived from Fotheringay,' he said.

Immediately an undercurrent of whispers ran around the hall: '*Fotheringay . . . Mary, Queen of Scots . . .*'

He asked for silence again. 'I must tell you that this morning, in the great hall of Fotheringay, the Queen of Scotland was put to death by the axe.'

There was an intake of breath from everyone in the hall.

'Long live the queen!' cried the speaker, and this sentiment was echoed in shocked voices by us all.

While we were all gathering our wits, a set of church bells began to ring out a celebratory peal. This was followed by others, so that within a few minutes our ears were beset by the pealing of bells right across the city. I looked for Tomas to ask what it all meant and what I should do, but he'd disappeared.

It was over an hour later before I found out more. After waiting in the hall feeling very out of place, I'd actually begun the journey home, terribly disappointed that I'd not been presented to Her Grace and, if the truth be told, wondering if my token of her appreciation might be quite lost to me now. My mind a tangle of questions, I'd walked as far as the Fleet and was about to cross it when I decided that I simply could *not* go on without speaking to someone and finding out exactly what had occurred, why the queen was so upset and what it all might mean for the country.

And so I turned back and came again to Whitehall Palace, this time not going to the banqueting hall, but rather to where I knew every scrap, every latest piece of news would be circulating: the servants' quarters. More particularly, I went towards the royal laundry and, saying once again I was Barbara's sister, gained entry.

Barbara was sitting with three other girls in the starching room and welcomed me in a very friendly manner. As I'd supposed, no one was a-bed, and little groups of servants were gathered, talking of the event in excited whispers. As each new piece of information arrived (from someone who knew a footman, was walking out with an equerry, or was the sister of one of the queen's night-servants) it was seized upon, marvelled at and duly passed around. Barbara's welcome to me became even warmer when she realised that I'd been in the hall at the time of the messenger's arrival and could provide first-hand information. When I'd satisfied everyone's curiosity as to the manner and demeanour of both the queen, the messenger and those about them, I asked why they thought the queen had screamed out so.

'Because she's furious!' Barbara answered straight.

I shook my head, still bewildered. 'But why?'

'Well, although she'd signed the death warrant, she didn't expect it to be used.'

'At least not straight away,' another girl added. 'She thought the matter would go again before her ministers.'

'She doesn't want the blood of an anointed queen on her hands,' continued Barbara.

'And now she's distraught! Her ladies are still with her . . . She's screaming and no one can calm her. She's blaming her ministers for forcing her to sign.'

'She says she never wished Mary put to death!' Barbara added.

I looked from one to the other of them. 'But . . . well, 'tis done now,' I said, shrugging.

'Aye,' Barbara said, 'and the whole country rejoices for it.'

'We are all free of the fear of Catholic rule!' said her friend.

'Twas a strange situation, I thought. The queen was upstairs in her palace, raging and sobbing by turns at the news (or so they said), while, below, we celebrated the very thing that she was so concerned about.

I stayed with Barbara and her friends a good while,

for no one seemed inclined to go to their bed. Someone lit a bonfire in the courtyard and the servants gathered around it, while a youth from the brewhouse brought ale to drink, and there was even dancing. 'Her Grace is safe!' people cried. 'Long live our beloved queen!'

After a glass of ale I began to feel very tired and, although there was still much laughter and gaiety, with church bells continuing to be rung across the city, thought to leave. Before I went, though, there was something I had to tell Barbara. I took her to one side, saying I wished to speak about my brother.

'You do?' I could not mistake the eagerness in her face. 'When might he be coming to see me?'

I shook my head. 'I'm afraid . . . not for many a long day.'

She frowned. 'Has he gone from London, then?'

'In a manner of speaking, yes, he has. He . . . he will come no more.' This was true, of course, because from now on, I'd have no time for acting with the players.

'He's *dead*?' she asked, shocked.

'No! Not that. He . . .' I bit my lip and tried again. 'You know I have undertaken some tasks for the queen's fool — a little spying work?'

She nodded, frowning.

'Well, I'm most sorry to tell you this, but part of this work required me to be disguised as a boy.'

'You dressed as a boy?' she repeated, perplexed.

I nodded. 'I, in fact, am my brother. We are one and the same person.' She still looked puzzled, so I added,

'There is no *brother*, only me.'

'Oh!' She suddenly blushed scarlet. 'But you . . . but I . . .'

'I am most truly sorry,' I said. 'I didn't mean to deceive you, merely sought you out as a friend. And then found it difficult to admit the truth because you . . . you . . .' my voice trailed away.

She didn't speak for some moments, then gave a small smile. ''Tis of no matter,' she said, 'for I have been exchanging smiles with a new 'prentice button-maker, and think he may ask me to go a-walking with him soon.'

'Then I'm very pleased for you,' I said, though I didn't know whether she'd spoken truly, or had just invented this button-maker to save face. We parted on very good terms, though, and said we'd see each other soon. Weary by then, I set off towards Green Lane, hoping that by the time I got as far as Ludgate it would be nigh on dawn and I'd be allowed into the city. Then it would just remain for me to face Mr Kelly and Dr Dee.

Chapter Twenty-One

I left the confines of the palace, crossed the Strand and went homewards, taking a shortcut down a narrow, dark passageway. Hearing a horse's hooves clattering on the cobbles behind me, I moved out of the way to allow it space, but to my surprise it was reined in. The rider jumped down and, to his credit, didn't seek to play a joke on me as he'd done so often before, but spoke out quickly.

'Lucy! Don't be alarmed. 'Tis only me.'

'Tomas!' I turned, most surprised. He was no longer dressed as a jester, but garbed much more soberly now, in dark suit and black cape with a hood. 'How did you find me?'

He smiled wryly. 'The whole of Whitehall Palace seems to be up and dancing a jig, and I had a hunch you wouldn't have gone home. I enquired in the laundries, and your friend Mistress Barbara said I'd just missed you. I thought to catch you at the city gates.'

'I'm happy you did,' I said. 'How was Her Grace when you left?'

'Still much out of sorts. First weeping, then angry, then sad, then weeping again. And no one can say anything to help or console her, for she has a ready answer each time. Even though . . .'

He hesitated and I prompted, 'Even though?'

'Even though she knows her life would never have been safe with the Scottish queen alive, and plots and counter-plots being discovered at every turn. Why, I attended Her Grace only last week and spent an hour trying to amuse her, but the whole time she sat staring into the distance, saying, *"Strike, or be struck . . . which shall it be?"* It was a matter that was much on her mind.'

I nodded. 'They are saying that although she wanted the Scottish queen dead, she didn't wish to take responsibility for it.'

'She did not. She wanted the deed done, but hoped that one of her ministers would undertake it and thus keep the blood from staining her hands.' He shook his head. 'No one was willing to do such a thing, however.'

We began walking together, the horse clip-clopping behind us. 'And with the death of the Scottish queen, what of Mistress Juliette?' I asked. 'Need we have bothered ourselves with her?'

Tomas nodded assuredly. ''Tis excellent news that she's out of the way, for our queen's enemies remain her enemies, even with Mary dead. All their efforts will now be focused on putting her son James on the throne.'

I hesitated, but could not resist asking if the late queen had gone to her death in a dignified and queenly manner, for this had been a question much asked about at the palace.

'She did,' Tomas answered, nodding. 'She was composed and calm, and carried a crucifix – or so said a third messenger who arrived after the others. She freely forgave her executioner, and prayed throughout her last moments in Latin.' He hesitated, then went on, 'When she removed her outer garments so as not to impede the axe, she was wearing a satin bodice and petticoat of scarlet, the colour of Catholic martyrdom.'

I was silent, thinking about this sad lady for a moment. I offered up a prayer for her soul, yet could not feel sorrow, for she'd been an enemy to our queen and would have usurped her if she could.

We neared Ludgate, where a small crowd of people had gathered, waiting to be allowed into the city. Some had obviously been out all night celebrating the news, others were peddlers with full trays, or goodwives with baskets of eggs ready to sell at the street markets. All were avidly discussing the happenings, for the royal story had crossed London in a trice.

Tomas looked to the east and pointed out the smudgy pink streaks in the sky. ''Tis not long until dawn,' he said. 'Are you cold?'

I was about to say no, but thought how nice it would be to have Tomas make a little fuss of me. I therefore affected a shiver or two until he, smiling, took off his cape and placed it around my shoulders. We looked into each other's eyes as he did so and – his face only an inch or two from mine – I held my breath. But then a hearty man with a fat piglet under each arm poked Tomas in the back, and the moment passed.

'We'll do well at market today, for people will be all for celebrating!' the man said. 'A roast suckling pig is an asset to any table, high or low. I only wish I had six of the beauties!'

'Indeed,' Tomas said politely, while I silently wished the man on the other side of the moon.

After that there were no more quiet moments, for two rival balladeers arrived at the gate, each with a pile of newly printed song-sheets selling at a penny each. One song was entitled *The joyful demise of the Queen of Scotland* and the other *Our gracious lady saved!* Each man set about singing his ballad with much gusto, causing several people living in the nearby houses to fling open their windows and shout a protest.

The sun came up, the streets grew lighter and more people arrived: sweeps, carpenters, milkmaids, carters, street-sellers and all the trades and, the gate being opened, we all went through. My feet trudged ever more slowly and Tomas offered to take me pillion on the horse but because that would have meant us reaching Green Lane more quickly, I refused. I didn't wish to say farewell to Tomas just yet, to have to explain myself to Dr Dee – or indeed want this strange night ever to end. We walked side by side, therefore, until the house came into view. Here Tomas tied the horse to a tree, gave a coin to a street-lad to mind it and said he'd accompany me to the door.

All was quiet upstairs and the curtains were closed, but downstairs I could hear – I was sure I could hear – Mistress Midge cursing as she swept the hallway.

'There's something I must say,' Tomas declared as we reached the front door, and before I had time to prepare myself for bad tidings, went on, 'I'm sorry I ever doubted you about Mistress Juliette, and I apologise for imagining that jealousy played a part in your actions. When I learned a little more about her, I should have taken you into my confidence. I'm sorry for that also.'

I dipped my head in acknowledgement – and forgave him, of course.

'And the other thing I have to say . . .' Tomas began, and just then the front door opened and Mistress Midge appeared with the house-broom and swept a flurry of dust into the street and over our shoes.

'Good Lord alive!' she said, looking at us, astonished. 'What are you doing out there so early?'

'I haven't come home yet,' I said.

'Of course!' She clapped her hand to her mouth. 'The Queen of Scotland! Is it true?'

'It is,' Tomas answered.

'Then that's rid of her and I'm blessed glad of it!' She gave our shoes a cursory brush-over with her broom and, after winking at me, went back inside.

We laughed at this, but then Tomas regained his serious manner. 'I'll wait here until Dr Dee rises,' he said. 'I must tell him that you've been out on the queen's business and ensure you're not in any way reprimanded. And one other thing . . .' He reached into the pocket of his breeches and pulled out a linen kerchief. 'I was with the Lord Chamberlain at some point last night; he had two or three little objects in his purse which the queen intended to present to those who'd served her well.'

I gave a gasp of excitement, for I hadn't thought he or anyone else would have remembered. 'I'm most honoured,' I said, and touched the bare spot at my neck where my groat had always hung. 'Is it a necklace?'

Tomas shook his head. ''Tis a ring.' He brought it out, gave it a little polish on his sleeve and handed it to me. 'It bears a little cameo of the queen, as you see.'

I stared at the pretty thing, delighted. 'Will you set it on my finger?' I asked.

Tomas nodded. I held out my left hand and he slipped it on the smallest finger. As he did so, an image suddenly came into my head: a church interior, viewed from above; a circular window of stained glass; shiny brasses set into the floor and blue and white flowers in tall vases. Tomas and I were standing before a black-clothed clerical gentleman, and Tomas was slipping a gold ring on to my wedding finger. So clear, so unexpected was this image that I clapped my hand to my mouth in surprise.

'What is it?' Tomas asked.

I blinked and the image disappeared. To be stored in my heart. ''Twas nothing,' I said, for there are some things that a maid should keep to herself.

'Your face is flushed, your cheeks have gone quite pink.'

I shook my head. 'I'm sure I don't know what you mean.'

Laughing, he pulled me towards him and kissed me full on the lips. This did not seem as if it was going to be a brief kiss, so I was venturing to kiss him back when the front door opened again, and there stood Merryl and Beth in the doorway in their nightdresses.

'Mistress Midge said . . .' Merryl began, then stopped, shocked, at the sight of us.

Beth gasped. 'So, is it true? *Is* Tomas your sweetheart? I think you ought to tell us.'

I stared at them, flustered, not really knowing what to say.

'Yes, he is,' Tomas said to them very amiably and sincerely. He glanced at me. 'That is, if she would like him to be.'

I nodded slowly, smiled and said, 'Yes, Tomas, she would like that very much.'

Some Historical Notes from the Author

The Queen and Her Suitors

This book is set in 1587, the year of the execution of Mary, Queen of Scots, but for dramatic purposes, some historical details surrounding this date have been changed. At this time, the start of the second half of Elizabeth I's reign, her ministers had not given up hope that she would marry and even, perhaps, provide the heir that England needed. Various suitors came from all over Europe and the

queen, while accepting their gifts and their professed love, played one off against the other, trying to gain the best deal for England and also foreign support in the event of a war. She actually exchanged rings with the French Duke of Anjou, but her ministers were not happy that she was marrying a Frenchman and a Catholic (also, he was seventeen years younger than her), so eventually it came to nothing. For the rest of her life the queen was to enjoy the company of men and always had her (usually younger) favourites.

Mary, Queen of Scots

Mary was cousin to the queen and had a good claim to the throne. She and her supporters were thorns in Elizabeth's side for most of her reign. Various plots to unseat the Protestant Elizabeth and replace her with the Catholic Mary were hatched and discovered (sometimes by one of Sir Francis Walsingham's team of spies) throughout Elizabeth's reign. A letter, signed by Mary, was discovered calling for Elizabeth's death (although Mary later said that the death threat was added after the letter had left her hands) and the queen was persuaded to sign her cousin's death warrant. When the execution was carried out, however, Elizabeth burst into a passion of crying and said that although she had signed the warrant, she had not meant to have it done.

Robert Dudley, Earl of Leicester

The queen showered titles on Robert Dudley, who was long held to be her lover (though no proof either way exists). Her ministers didn't approve of him, however, calling him 'the Gypsy' because he was brown from being in the open air and was comparatively low-born. His first wife died in strange circumstances and then, some years later, he got tired of being kept on a string by Elizabeth, and married the Countess of Essex, one of the royal ladies-in-waiting. No courtiers were quite brave enough to tell Elizabeth of this, and tradition has it that she was eventually informed of it by one of her thwarted suitors in a fit of jealousy. The newly-weds were banned from court immediately and, although the queen later relented and allowed Robert Dudley back, she never received his wife, whom she nicknamed 'the she-wolf'.

The Real Dr Dee

Dr Dee was a mathematician, linguist and scholar – but it seems that he was also very gullible. Kelly, his 'scryer', purported to speak to angels who gave him details of how to turn base metal into gold (by using the so-called 'philosopher's stone'), but unfortunately these details were in a strange angelic language which could never be properly deciphered. Dr Dee spent most of his life waiting for the queen to endow him with a proper title and a paid position, but this never happened. Apart from a spell in Poland, he lived in Mortlake next to the church, where he owned a huge library of books on matters magical, spiritual and mathematic. He was born in 1527 and died in 1608 (five years after the queen), reportedly penniless. Some say that Dr Dee lives on in Shakespeare's portrayal of Prospero, the magician in *The Tempest*, probably written in 1610.

The Ladies-in-Waiting

These ladies, and the more intimate maids of honour, formed an elegant and decorative backdrop to the person of the queen, providing support, entertainment, advice and good company for Her Grace. Girls from titled families sometimes entered the Court aged about twelve and, after serving the queen for a number of years, were found suitable husbands. The queen, being unmarried herself, didn't approve of marriage for all, however, and was known to punish her ladies by sending them temporarily to the Tower of London if they fell in love with someone she didn't approve of – or someone whose attentions she wanted for herself.

The Elizabethan Court

The Court exercised a magnetic attraction for people; courtiers were the A-list celebrities of the day. It was the centre of affairs, the very heart of patronage and power. People visiting would spend a fortune on their outfits in the hopes of being noticed; being spoken to by Her Grace was the ultimate accolade.

The queen and her Court moved palaces every few months in order that the buildings could be aired and freshened after their occupation. In summer, they also went 'on progress', visiting the houses of the wealthiest subjects, who would spend an astonishing amount of money refurbishing, rebuilding and providing extravagant diversions and attractions: plays, masques, music, fireworks, bear-baiting, jousting and dancing, in order to entertain the queen and her Court. One titled courtier even dug up his grounds to provide a lake for a lavish water pageant, which featured little boats sailing between miniature islands.

The Banqueting Hall at Whitehall

As if the hundreds of rooms that the palace contained were not enough, in 1581 Elizabeth ordered the construction of a 'canvas and wood' temporary banqueting hall. (In Tudor times, 'banqueting' meant the final dainty sweetmeats you would eat after a meal.) The building sounded very beautiful; garlanded with swags of flowers, decorated with trees in tubs and lit by candles. In 1609 King James had it replaced by a permanent structure, but this burned down ten years later.

Playgoing

The Theatre and the Curtain at Shoreditch opened around 1576 and are generally held to be the first theatres in England. They proved popular, and several companies were formed to act in them, including the Queen's Men, the Lord Chamberlain's Men (Shakespeare's company) and the Admiral's Men. They all poached each other's best players and most popular plays. Shakespeare was probably not in London at this time but *The Two Gentlemen of Verona* and *The Taming of the Shrew* were held to be his first plays, written in the late 1580s. James Burbage was a leading actor-manager and theatre owner, and was succeeded by his son Richard, who became even more famous. Until Charles II came to the throne, there were, of course, no female actors.

Mistress Midge's Mice Recipe

A typical sixteenth-century gingerbread recipe would have consisted of stale white bread-crumbs mixed with grated ginger and red wine, moulded into shapes and dried in a warm oven. This is a modern version.

Ingredients:
- ❖ 110 g margarine
- ❖ 100 g sugar
- ❖ 120 ml black treacle
- ❖ 1 egg yolk

- ❖ 250 g plain flour, sifted
- ❖ 2 g baking powder
- ❖ 1 g ground cinnamon
- ❖ 2 g ground cloves
- ❖ 2 g ground nutmeg
- ❖ 2 g ground ginger

For decoration:
- ❖ Currants
- ❖ String

Directions:

1. In a large bowl, cream together the margarine and sugar until smooth.
2. Stir in the treacle and egg yolk.
3. Combine all the other ingredients and blend into the black treacle mixture until smooth.
4. Cover and chill the dough for at least one hour.
5. Preheat the oven to 175 °C (350 °F / gas mark 4).
6. On a lightly floured surface, roll the dough out to 5 mm thick.
7. Cut the dough into mouse shapes, add currants for eyes and string for tails.
8. Bake 8-10 minutes on greased baking sheets in the preheated oven, until firm.
9. Remove the mice from the baking sheets to cool on wire racks.

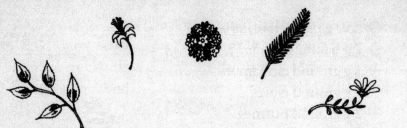

Tussy-Mussies

These sweetly scented nosegays were popular accessories in the sixteenth century, when ladies would carry them to sniff if confronted with any foul smells. Some even believed that breathing through the mixture of flowers and herbs would keep the owner from breathing in germs or disease and act as a plague preventative. Later, tussy-mussies were given amongst friends for the meanings bestowed on individual plants (for instance, using scarlet geraniums denoted 'comfort').

To make:

A suitable tussy-mussy for a maiden would be a central bloom of a large pink rose (pure and lovely) encircled with contrasting flowers and leaves of mint (virtue), sage (domestic virtue), forget-me-nots (true love), golden marjoram (blushes), lime blossom (conjugal love) and rosemary (remembrance).

Bind the stems with florist's tape as you go to keep the posy tight and finish the edges with a large-leafed herb (like lady's mantle) to emphasise the round shape.

Glossary

coffer – a box or chest for keeping valuables

coxcomb – a foppish fellow; a conceited dandy

equerry – an officer in the royal household

farthingale – a hoop or framework worn under skirts to shape and spread them

frowsy – unkempt; of shabby appearance

galliard – an athletic dance characterised by leaps, hops and jumps. A favourite dance of Elizabeth I

gee-gaw – decorative trinket; a bauble

groat – English silver coin worth four old pence, used from the fourteenth century to the seventeenth century

harridan – a woman with a reputation for being a scold or a nag

horn book – early primer showing alphabet, etc., consisting of a wooden board protected by a thin sheet of cattle horn

kennel – a rough drainage channel for street waste-water and rubbish

kirtle – the skirt part of a woman's outfit. During this time everything (skirt, bodice, sleeves and ruff) came separately and were pinned together during dressing

litter – a man-powered form of transport, consisting of a chair or couch enclosed by curtains and carried on a frame or poles

lying-in – the period just before and after a woman's confinement during childbirth

malmsey – a sweet wine

marchpane – the old word for marzipan

masque – festive courtly entertainment which might include singing, dancing or acting

pattens – overshoes held on to feet by leather bands to elevate the feet and aid walking in the mud

porringer – a shallow dish or cup, usually with a handle, and used for eating soup, stews or porridge

prink up – to dress oneself finely; to deck out and preen oneself

Rhenish – a dry white wine

ribband – a ribbon

scry – to see or divine, especially by crystal-gazing

simples – medicines made from herbs

sucket – a type of sweet, typically orange or lemon slices, sugared and crystallised

tilt – a type of joust played by armoured combatants mounted on horseback

tiring room – the dressing room of a theatre, probably deriving from 'attiring room'

vittles – food; also spelled *victuals*

Bibliography

Bremness, Lesley, *DK Pocket Encyclopedia of Herbs*
Dorling Kindersley, 1990

Dickson, Andrew, *The Rough Guide to Shakespeare*
Rough Guides, 2005

Fell Smith, Charlotte, *John Dee 1527-1608*
Constable and Company, 1909

Hibbert, Christopher and Weinreb, Ben, *The London Encyclopedia*
Book Club Associates, 1983

Jenkins, Elizabeth, *Elizabeth the Great*
Phoenix Press, 1958

Picard, Liza, *Elizabeth's London*
Phoenix, 2003

Weir, Alison, *Elizabeth the Queen*
Pimlico, 1999

Williams, Neville, *The Life and Times of Elizabeth I*
Book Club Associates, 1972

Woolley, Hannah, *The Gentlewoman's Companion (1675)*
Prospect Books, 2001

If you enjoyed this book, why not try the following,
also by Mary Hooper

At The Sign Of The

Sugared Plum

Read on for a tantalising extract . . .

Hannah is excited as she embarks on her first ever trip
to the capital to help sister Sarah in her sweetmeats
shop. But she does not get the warm welcome she
expected. Sarah is horrified that Hannah did not get
her message to stay away – the Plague is taking hold
of London.

Chapter One

The first week of June, 1665

*'June 7th. The hottest day that ever I felt
in my life . . .'*

To tell the truth, I was rather glad to get away from Farmer Price and his rickety old cart. He made me uneasy with his hog's breath and his red, sweaty face and the way he'd suddenly bellow out laughing at nothing at all. I was uneasy, too, about something he'd said when I'd told him I was going to London to join my sister Sarah in her shop.

'You be going to live in the City, Hannah?' he'd asked, pushing his battered hat up over his forehead. 'Wouldn't think you'd want to go there.'

'Oh, but I do!' I'd said, for I'd been set on living in London for as long as I could remember. 'I'm fair desperate to reach the place.'

'Times like this . . . thought your sister would try and keep you away.'

'No, she sent for me specially,' I'd said, puzzled. 'Her shop is doing well and she wants my help in it. I'm to be trained in the art of making sweetmeats,'

I'd added.

'Sweetmeats is it?' He'd given one of his bellows. 'That's comfits for corpses, then!'

He left me in Southwarke on the south bank of the Thames, and I thanked him, slipped down from his cart and – remembering to take my bundle and basket from the back – began to walk down the crowded road towards London Bridge.

As the bridge came into view I stopped to draw breath, putting down my baggage but being careful to keep my things close by, for I'd been warned often enough about the thieving cutpurses and murderous villains who thronged the streets of London. I straightened my skirts and flounced out my petticoat to show off the creamy ruff of lace I'd sewn onto it – Sarah had told me that petticoats were now worn to be seen – then pushed down my hair to try and flatten it. This was difficult for, to my great vexation, it stuck out as curly as the tails of piglets and was flame red. Nothing I wore, be it hat, hood or cap, could contain it. I pulled my new white cap down tightly, however, and tied the ribbons into a tidy bow under my chin. I hoped I looked a pleasant and comely sight walking across into the city, and that no one would look at me and realise that I was a newly arrived country girl.

It was a hot day even though it was only the first of June, and all the hotter for me because I was wearing several layers of clothes. This wasn't because I'd - misjudged the weather, more because I knew that whatever I didn't wear, I'd have to carry. I had on then: a cambric shift, two petticoats, a dark linsey-woolsey skirt and a linen blouse. Over these was a short jacket which had been embroidered by my mother, and a dark woollen shawl lay across my shoulders.

I'd been studying the people carefully as we'd neared the bridge, hoping that I might see my friend Abigail, who'd come from our village last year to be a maid in one of the big houses, and also hoping to see some great lady, a person of quality, so I could judge how well I stood against her regarding fashion. There was no sign of Abby, however, and most of the quality were in sedan chairs or carriages, with only the middling and poorer sort on foot. These folk were wearing a great variety of things: men were in tweedy country clothes, rough working worsteds or the severely cut suits and white collars of the Puritans, the women wearing everything from costly velvet down to poor rags that my mother would have scorned to use as polishing cloths for the pewter.

'That's a fine red wig you've got there, lass!' a young male voice said, and I realised that I'd paused beside a brewhouse.

I turned indignantly on the speaker. 'It's not a wig. It's my own hair!' I said to the two men – one young and one old – who were leaning against the wall, mugs of ale in their hands.

'And fine patches across your nose, too,' said the elder.

I opened my mouth to say more and then realised that the youth and man outside the Gown and Claret were making fun of me.

'They're not patches, William, they're called sun kisses!' the first said, and they both roared with laughter.

I picked up my basket, feeling my cheeks go pink.

At The Sign Of The Sugared Plum
AVAILABLE NOW